There was something about Annie... something Prince Johann just couldn't let go.

Three more steps and he was directly in front of her. She tilted her face up toward his, her lips parted temptingly. Annie shivered.

"Cold?" he asked her.

"Not exactly."

"You want to give up?"

"Never." She smiled.

For a fleeting moment he thought he could fall in love with her. If he was the type to fall in love, that was. But he wasn't.

Elizabeth Harbison has been an avid reader for as long as she can remember. After devouring the Nancy Drew and Trixie Beldon series in school, she moved on to the suspense of Mary Stewart, Dorothy Eden and Daphne du Maurier, just to name a few. From there it was a natural progression to writing, although early efforts have been securely hidden away in the back of a wardrobe.

Elizabeth lives in Maryland with her husband, John, and daughter Mary Paige, as well as two dogs, Bailey and Zuzu. She loves to hear from readers and you can write to her c/o Box 1636, Germantown, MD 20875, USA.

Recent titles by the same author:

EMMA AND THE EARL
PLAIN JANE MARRIES THE BOSS

ANNIE AND THE PRINCE

BY
ELIZABETH HARBISON

MILLS & BOON®

To two of the finest men who ever walked this earth:
John Edward McShulskis (1932-1983)
and
John Anthony McShulskis (1910-1998)
Lives well lived.
I'm so proud to have had such great men as my father and grandfather.

DID YOU PURCHASE THIS BOOK WITHOUT A COVER?

If you did, you should be aware it is **stolen property** as it was reported *unsold and destroyed* by a retailer. Neither the author nor the publisher has received any payment for this book.

All the characters in this book have no existence outside the imagination of the author, and have no relation whatsoever to anyone bearing the same name or names. They are not even distantly inspired by any individual known or unknown to the author, and all the incidents are pure invention.

All Rights Reserved including the right of reproduction in whole or in part in any form. This edition is published by arrangement with Harlequin Enterprises II B.V. The text of this publication or any part thereof may not be reproduced or transmitted in any form or by any means, electronic or mechanical, including photocopying, recording, storage in an information retrieval system, or otherwise, without the written permission of the publisher.

This book is sold subject to the condition that it shall not, by way of trade or otherwise, be lent, resold, hired out or otherwise circulated without the prior consent of the publisher in any form of binding or cover other than that in which it is published and without a similar condition including this condition being imposed on the subsequent purchaser.

MILLS & BOON and MILLS & BOON with the Rose Device are registered trademarks of the publisher.

First published in Great Britain 2001
Harlequin Mills & Boon Limited,
Eton House, 18-24 Paradise Road, Richmond, Surrey TW9 1SR

© Elizabeth Harbison 2000

ISBN 0 263 82600 7
Set in Times Roman 10½ on 12¼ pt.
02-0601-42320

Printed and bound in Spain
by Litografia Rosés, S.A., Barcelona

Prologue

"Oh, Annie, I can't believe you're going! Are you sure this is the right thing to do? Quitting your job and just taking off for Europe this way?"

Annie Barimer looked at her friend, Joy Simon, who worked in the admissions office at Pendleton School for Girls. Annie, until this very moment, had been the school librarian there for five years. "I'm sure, Joy," she said, without a trace of the melancholy Joy had etched all over her face. "Besides, I'm not just 'taking off for Europe', as you well know. I'm going to travel for one short week." It was hard to contain her glee. France! Germany! She was *finally* going to the places she'd wanted to see for so long. The week would pass very fast. "Then I go to Kublenstein and start my new job."

"For strangers." Joy sniffed dramatically and took another piece of the sheet cake the staff had bought for Annie's farewell party. She scooped some soupy ice cream onto the paper plate. "Who knows what they're like? They may be a family of psycho killers."

"They are the daughters of Marie de la Fuenza," Annie corrected.

"Right. And what do we know about her?"

"We know that twenty years ago she attended Pendleton for the full four years and that her mother also attended. Plus her family virtually paid for the library." She raised an eyebrow at Joy. "I think we can trust them."

Joy wasn't convinced. "You've got to admit they've been a little cryptic about the job. It's always the daughters of Marie de la Fuenza. What's her married name? What are the daughters' names? Why is everything addressed through the embassy in Kublenstein instead of a home address? Where *is* Kublenstein anyway?"

"It's in the Alps," Annie answered, refusing to be troubled by Joy's other admittedly good points. "And her husband is an important figure in the government there or something, so everything is being arranged very carefully."

Joy shrugged. "Well, I still don't see what's wrong with staying right here at Pendleton."

"I've been wanting to go to Europe all my life but this is the first chance I've ever gotten to actually go live there for awhile and get paid for it." Pictures of the Eiffel Tower, Notre Dame, the Parthenon, the Colosseum and a million other grand European landmarks danced in her head. The dreary little town of

Pendleborough couldn't compare on any level. "I wouldn't miss this for anything."

"Somehow I knew you'd say that."

Annie laughed and pulled back a tendril of coffee-colored hair that had escaped from her braid and kept tickling her cheek. "I've only said it a thousand times." A couple of teachers from the math department walked past, patted her shoulder and wished her luck. She thanked them and turned back to Joy and the conversation at hand. "Look, this is a dream come true. Be happy for me."

Joy raised her hands in front of her. "All right, all right. To be honest, I'm not worried about you in Europe at all, I'm worried about me, here. I'm going to be bored out of my mind when you're gone."

"I'll write," Annie told her sincerely. She imagined herself printing the Pendleton address on an envelope from thousands of miles away. The idea made her feel giddy, even though Joy would prefer the immediacy of e-mail. "I promise."

Joy put a piece of cake into her mouth and nodded. "That's what you say now." She held up a finger, swallowed, then added, "But what happens when you find your Prince Charming over there and get so wrapped up in a romance that you forget about writing, hmm?"

"So *that's* where Prince Charming is," Annie said, with mock surprise. "Stupid me, I've been kissing frogs on the wrong side of the Atlantic for twenty-five years."

Joy raised an eyebrow. "Laugh if you want to, but I have a feeling you're going to meet someone there.

Someone romantically significant. You might never come back!''

Annie was sure Joy couldn't have been further off the mark. She couldn't even imagine meeting the man of her dreams overseas and never coming back...though the idea had some appeal as a fantasy. ''You're right that I'll be meeting someone. Actually, two someones. Marie de la Fuenza's daughters. I hate to disillusion you, but I'm going to have no time for any kind of social life at all.'' It was true. Even if she was the extroverted type who'd go out and meet people to party with, she wasn't going to have time for it with this job.

''Remember that tarot card reading I did for you?'' Joy asked. ''It said you were going to meet a very important and powerful man. That card was in the love position.''

Annie thought about it, then recalled what her friend was talking about. ''Joy, that was just a prank for the school fair. Surely you don't believe in any of that stuff. For heaven's sake, you were reading it right out of a book.''

''That doesn't mean it wasn't true. Besides, my psychic feelings have been right before,'' Joy said, hurt.

''When?''

''I told you Judy Gallagher was pregnant.''

It was on the tip of Annie's tongue to point out that everyone had realized Judy was pregnant as soon as she started bolting from her first period Social Studies class for the bathroom every morning. Instead, Annie gave a concessionary nod. "That's true, you did."

"And I'm right about this, too. You mark my words."

"Duly marked."

"Besides, you need to meet a guy. You need to have someone to support you in a year when your job tutoring English ends and you're out of work."

"It's not always that easy to find someone."

Joy sighed. "So…what are you wearing on the plane?"

Annie laughed. Joy's greatest pleasure in life, next to food, was fashion. And she was quite good at it, too, if not exactly a willowy fashion plate herself.

"I'm wearing this," Annie answered, indicating the comfy cotton sweater and leggings she was wearing.

"Honestly, you have this great figure and you never do anything to emphasize it. It's so unfair. Maybe you should take me along to advise you."

"I'm sure I should."

There was a faint honking outside the door. Annie moved to look out the window. A yellow cab had pulled up in the courtyard in front of the library building.

"Cab's here," someone called, just as Annie saw it.

"Time to go, I guess."

"Looks like it," Joy said miserably.

Annie couldn't commiserate. Her heart felt as light as air. In fact, it was fluttering just like a bird from the excitement. This wasn't regular anticipation. Annie was feeling like her whole life was about to change forever.

Could there possibly be something to Joy's prediction?

She took a steady breath and gave Joy a kiss on the cheek. "Don't look so sad. I promised I would write to you and I will."

"You better. Have you got the digital camera I gave you?"

"All packed."

"Good. Take pictures. E-mail them to me. You remember how I showed you?"

"I remember." Annie moved to get in the back seat, waving to the people who had congregated to watch her go.

"And don't forget to tell me all about *him*," Joy added significantly.

Annie's face warmed. As soon as the cab drove away, people would pounce on Joy to find out what that comment had meant. Oh, well, let them. Maybe she even preferred it that way.

After all, this was the end of Annie—Boring Librarian and the beginning of Annie—Woman of the World.

Chapter One

Why was she feeling so apprehensive? Annie wondered. She sighed and leaned against the train window, watching the Alpine countryside whip by as they sped toward Lassberg, the capital of the tiny European country of Kublenstein. True, things hadn't worked out well with her hotel in Paris, and Germany had turned out to be more expensive than she could afford. But now she was headed to Kublenstein two days earlier than expected so she could get the lay of the land before meeting her new employers.

It would be nice. She hadn't been on a real vacation since she was six and had gone to a local amusement park a couple of towns over from her Maryland home. Since high school she'd just been treading water, working to stay afloat and to pay the never-ending cycle of bills. All of that would change, now. She had a good job in what was apparently a wonderful household in Europe. It was just what she'd always dreamed of.

But as the train rails rattled under her feet, she dissected her plan for the hundredth time and couldn't see one thing in it that should make her stomach feel like it was full of bats.

The train lurched and a young man with pale blond hair and a large rucksack on his back knocked against her, spilling hot drops of coffee on her blouse. "Very sorry, ma'am," he said, with a light Scandinavian accent.

"It's okay," she said quietly, but he had already moved on, not having waited for a response. She pushed her heavy reading glasses back up the bridge of her nose and rummaged through her bag for a tissue. She hated being called ma'am, especially by people who were only a few years younger than she was. And how did he know to speak English? She must look very American.

She dabbed at the coffee with a sigh. The stain remained. She balled the tissue up, put it in the trash receptacle, and tried to return her attention to the book in her lap, but it was difficult. The train was noisy and hot, and so humid that the air almost felt damp against her skin. The coffee stain did.

After one or two unsuccessful tries to concentrate on the book in her hand, she set it back down in her lap and let her mind wander to more familiar thoughts of home. If she'd stayed, she'd be in her small, chilly apartment now, watching the news and eating leftover Chinese food. In the morning, her alarm would go off at 6:50 a.m. and she'd shower and drive to work. Not that that was totally unful-filling. As librarians went, she was an exceptionally good one. She always enjoyed helping students find more creative ways to look at their assignments. She encouraged them to take the harder route in order to learn more and she loved to help them find strong role models in heroic characters from literature.

Unfortunately, at Pendleton that was often consid-ered 'pushing the envelope' and she'd been told more than once by members of the very conservative board of directors to leave the teaching to the teachers.

It was distinctly possible that if she hadn't re-signed when she did the board would have asked the headmaster, Lawrence Pegrin, to dismiss her. Lawrence had had some stern words for her about her tutoring methods more than once, though she sus-pected he secretly approved. In fact, when Marie de la Fuenza's husband had contacted the school look-ing for a suitable English tutor and nanny, Lawrence had suggested Annie without hesitation. In a private conversation he'd assured her that if it didn't work out she could return to Pendleton, regardless of what the board of directors wished.

That was some comfort, though not quite enough to make her relax now. It was almost as if she was having some sort of premonition, but she couldn't decipher it. Was something horrible about to happen? Or something wonderful? It was such a fine line be-tween excitement and fear.

Looking at the passing scenery, Annie thought if a fairy tale could come true, this would be the place for it. The mountains stretched high toward the steel-gray sky, huge triangles of shadow and snow. Ancient evergreens with white snow fingertips stood indomitably, as they had done for thousands of years. It was a landscape for the Brothers Grimm, as dreamy as clouds, yet with a healthy hint of the gothic snaking through the hazy shadows of the deep woodlands.

As the miles of icy black forest rolled by she looked around at the other coach passengers. There seemed to be thousands of them, and at least half looked like college students, faces aglow with the excitement of travel and with voices loud and enthusiastic.

Suddenly Annie felt claustrophobic from it all. If she had to stay in this hot, crowded car for one more moment she'd stop breathing. She decided to see if there was another car farther up with fewer people.

She shoved her book into her bag, got up and hauled her two suitcases onto the link between cars where there was a tiny bathroom. The air was cooler immediately. She'd rather stand here for the rest of the trip than go back to the crowded coach car, though it was probably against the rules. Unfortunately, she'd have to shlep her heavy bags with her through the cars until she found someplace else to sit.

But first she was going to try to get rid of the still-damp coffee stain on her shirt. She slipped into the minute bathroom and wedged the door open with her foot so she could keep an eye on her bags. The stiff paper towels were practically water resistant, but she was able to get most of the coffee out of the fabric.

What was left, she noted with a sigh, was a huge collection of watermarks.

She stepped out of the bathroom and went to an open window between the cars and breathed in the frigid air. She took another deep breath and hoisted up her bags again, opening the door to the next car with her shoulder. It was strangely empty and deliciously quiet. She realized immediately it was a first-class car. The private cubicles were tempting with their closed doors, cushioned seats, and tiny wall lights giving off a warm glow against the chill gray landscape outside. It was impossible to resist. On impulse, she decided to go into one of the compartments and languish there as a first-class passenger until they got to Lassberg or until someone kicked her out. After all, it wasn't like stealing. If she didn't use one, it would just go on being empty.

Suddenly she noticed an extraordinarily handsome man in the compartment before her. He was alone. It was obvious no one was coming back to sit with him. Something about his posture suggested detachment. Isolation. She craned her neck to try and see his hands. No ring, just as she'd guessed.

She caught her breath. If only she were the type of woman a man like this would look at twice. Dreamer, she chastised herself. She hadn't been the type to catch a man's eye in all of her twenty-five years, and it wasn't likely to happen now, especially with an Adonis like the one she was looking at.

Still, she had been swept up in the fairy-tale atmosphere of the Alps and the memory of Joy's prediction. Why not go with it, just for another moment?

She touched her finger to the door. ''Maybe you'd be my Prince Charming,'' she said under her breath, her words fogging the glass. ''If fairy godmothers really existed.'' She gave a slight laugh. ''And if it wasn't so heinous for a modern woman to want a Prince Charming.''

The man's profile, illuminated by the little orange glow of the reading lights, was arresting. The nose was straight and long, his cheekbones beautifully pronounced and his jaw was square and strong. His gleaming hair was as dark as Heathcliff's in *Wuthering Heights.* She couldn't tell what color his eyes were, but the lashes were long and dark and she was certain his expression was brooding.

On the surface he looked like an ordinary guy, wearing an old pair of jeans and a ragged wool sweater. It seemed a little strange that he was in first class—he could almost have passed for one of the students in the other car except that he was older. There was a regal quality about him that gave Annie the impression that he was right at home in the elegant accommodations.

Clack clack sheesh clack clack sheesh, the train rumbled beneath her feet racing across the miles of picturesque countryside. The door to his compartment was open just a crack. Someone with more nerve than Annie would have walked right in and sat down.

She nearly laughed at the very idea of herself doing something like that. It was completely unlike her. If she did it, if she could gather enough nerve just to go for it, it would be baptism by fire, but—

"Excuse me, miss, may I have your ticket please?" a cheery, loud German voice called behind her.

She whirled around to face a short, round, uniformed railroad employee. One hand was filled with passenger tickets that he'd already collected, his other hand was extended toward Annie expectantly.

"Yes…I…" Her face flamed as she thought, for one wild moment, that he might have known what she'd been contemplating. She fumbled awkwardly through her purse, looking for the first-class ticket she knew wasn't in there and hoping for the coach-class ticket that should have been. She switched from English to German and said, "One moment. It's in here somewhere."

She glanced up and the train employee lowered his brow.

"Really." She dug some more, feeling more hopeless by the second of ever finding the ticket. "I bought it right before I got on board in Munich." She prayed silently that the Greek god in the private compartment wasn't watching. He probably was, after all the door to his compartment was nearly all glass and she was right in front of it.

The train conductor shifted his weight and crossed his arms in front of him. "Come now, miss, you can purchase your ticket on board. It's four hundred marks."

Annie felt her blood drain to her feet. "Four hundred—" The train suddenly lurched and she lost her balance, teetering momentarily against the door to the mystery man's compartment before it flew open, sending her sprawling onto the hard metal floor in front of the man himself, her glasses clattering on the floor beside her.

"I'm sorry." Annie felt around for her glasses and, finding them, put them on. She met the man's eyes, which were green and even more intense than she possibly could have imagined, and mentally shrank to about two inches tall.

The man shifted in his seat, watching with what appeared to be some interest. Those incredible eyes flicked from her to the angry-looking train official and back again, but he said nothing.

"I'm so sorry." Annie scrambled to her feet, and tried to smile.

He smiled back and cocked his head slightly, as if questioning what she did for an encore. "Quite all right," he said smoothly.

He took her breath away and made her lose all track of what she was going to say. "I was…"

The train employee cleared his throat, an unpleasant reminder of the other presence in the compartment.

She turned to him and said, "I've got my ticket here someplace."

Both men looked at her, so she made another attempt at finding her ticket in her bag. It was nowhere to be seen. In English, she muttered a mild oath that would, nevertheless, have gotten a student at Pendleton sent to the headmaster's office.

The ticket collector frowned. "I'm afraid you'll have to purchase a ticket, miss."

"She said she has a ticket already," the other man said, in a voice as rich and smooth as crème brûlée. His German was slightly accented, but Annie couldn't tell what the inflection was.

"Policy, sir." The little round face grew redder. "I don't make the rules, I just enforce them."

"That won't be necessary," the Adonis said. He hesitated for a moment, then reached for a small leather backpack at his feet. He nodded at Annie. "Please, allow me." He pulled out several large-denomination bills.

"No, no, I can't let you do that," Annie objected, digging in her purse for the four hundred marks.

"But I insist." Her unlikely hero gave a cold nod to the other man. "Please bring her bags in here." He started to hand some bills to the man but Annie, who had been hurriedly counting out the four hundred, handed her money to him first. "Thank you anyway," she said to the Adonis.

He held her eyes steadily, just a touch of a smile on his lips. "Certainly."

The rail employee started to speak, but his mouth shut suddenly and he poked his head forward to study Annie's knight more closely. "Wait a minute... Don't tell me you're—"

The man looked down suddenly, like a reflex. "Thank you so much for your help. That will be all." With that dismissal, he looked away, heedless of the ticket collector's stare.

The train worker left, scratching his head, and

muttering, "Of course it's not him, he wouldn't be here," without even a glance back at Annie.

Annie studied the man wondering who the conductor had thought her companion was. He kept his face slightly averted. Whoever it was that he looked like, he didn't seem to want to talk about it. Probably some obscure European movie star. He certainly had the looks for it. More to the point, he was turning her insides to melted butter, and she'd better stop gawking at him.

"Thank you for your offer of help," she said, and began to back toward the door. "I apologize for this intrusion on your privacy."

He gave a shrug. "It's no problem. I'm only sorry that man was such an unpleasant ambassador to my country. You are American?"

She stopped and nodded, wondering if he expected her to stay.

"Please," he said, answering her unasked question with a wave of his hand. "Have a seat. I'd welcome the company, unless you have someplace else you have to be."

"N-no. Thank you." She sat, mesmerized by him.

"I wouldn't want you to take home the impression that Kublenstein is unfriendly to strangers," he said, with a devastating smile.

"I won't, I absolutely won't," she said. There was a moment's silence, so she added, "I really do have a ticket, or at least I did…"

"I believe you."

But she wasn't sure if he really believed her or

not. "My name is Annie, by the way." He didn't answer right away, so she prodded him, "And you are…?"

He watched her for a moment, wearing an expression she couldn't quite read. "You don't know?" he asked after a long minute.

A tickle ran over her skin, like a cool breeze. It was a feeling she'd had before, always when something big was about to happen. She had that sense now, that his question held more significance than it appeared to. "No," she said simply. "Should I?"

He smiled. "No, of course not. I simply thought I'd—I'd already said." He shrugged, but looked suspiciously like the cat that ate the canary. He extended his hand to her. "I am Hans."

She took his hand, smiling at the warmth of his touch. Joy's premonition of her meeting someone came to mind again and she nearly laughed. Well, in a way, Joy had been right. "It's nice to meet you."

He kept his grasp on her hand, seemingly distracted. "Believe me," he said, his smile broadening. "The pleasure is all mine."

Suddenly she was overwhelmed by his handsomeness and the intensity with which he leveled his gaze at her. She looked down and cleared her throat. "I have to say, I'm not normally so clumsy…or so careless as to lose my ticket. It must be jet lag or something. It's my first time in Europe."

"Really?" He sounded genuinely surprised. "Your German is quite good."

She felt a flush rise in her cheeks. "Thanks. My

grandmother was German and she spoke it to me for the first five years of my life.'' She was rambling. She always rambled when she was nervous. ''I've wanted to come visit her homeland for as long as I can remember.''

''I see.'' He nodded thoughtfully. ''So why have you decided to visit now?''

''First, I finally had enough money saved up to come. I almost wasn't able to do it at all, but then I got a job and…'' She let her voice trail off, realizing she was starting to ramble again. ''Anyway, here I am.''

''Here you are.'' He continued to look at her in a way that made her squirm.

A short silence filled the car.

Annie had an inexplicable urge to fill it. ''You know, I really don't know how I lost my ticket. I put it with my passport in this secure zipper pouch right here—'' she lifted her purse and unzipped the side ''—so I could be very sure where they were. There must be a hole or something—oh.'' She pulled the ticket out of the pocket and felt her face grow hot. ''That's strange. Why on earth wasn't it there before?'' Annie was seriously disconcerted. She'd searched the pocket thoroughly. It was almost like magic.

When she looked up, Hans was wearing a questioning expression.

''I know this looks strange, but I really didn't do it on purpose.''

He looked amused. ''I wouldn't think so.''

An awkward silence stretched between them and after a few moments Annie asked, "So…are you stopping in Lassberg?"

"I am." He nodded, eyeing her. His words sounded careful. "I live there."

"How lucky for you. It's a lovely countryside."

"Yes, I agree."

She looked out at a mountain ski run. "Do you do a lot of skiing, living here?"

He shook his head. "Unfortunately, I don't get out that much. My…work…prevents it."

She looked at him and smiled. "You're out now."

"I am, but it's for business. Every month or so I take a trip like this into the countryside for a few days, but even then I don't take much time for recreation."

Annie would have given anything for a job that involved such a lovely perk as train trips across the Alps. "What is it you do?"

He hesitated, then said, "I work for the civil service. It's not very interesting. What about you?" It was a slightly abrupt change of subject. "Are you going to be vacationing in Lassberg?"

"Well, for a couple of days. After that…" Perhaps because of her fatigue, Annie found herself wishing he'd ask her out. She immediately brought her fantasy into check. She didn't even know the man. He was a stranger on a train. With that in mind, she didn't go on to tell him she'd be taking a job as a private English tutor in Lassberg in a few days.

"After that…?" he prompted.

She hesitated. ''I'm just going to vacation here for a couple of days.'' She shrugged. ''Then it's back to work.''

But as Annie settled back into her seat in the first-class compartment, and looked at the handsome stranger across from her, it wasn't her new job that made her smile. Instead, it was the thought that maybe Joy's prediction of finding her own Prince Charming just might turn out to be true.

Chapter Two

Prince Ludwig Johann Ambrose George of Kublenstein, known to the public and the press as Prince Johann, and to a select few as Hans, leaned back against the stiff leather seat of the train to study the woman before him.

She was very attractive, though she was doing everything she could not to show it. Her glossy dark hair was pulled back into a tight braid in the back. He couldn't help but imagine taking her hair out of the braid and running his fingers slowly through it. It would be soft, he knew, and probably smelled of flowers. He focused on her eyes, looking for the vivid blue he'd glimpsed there when her glasses had slipped off. They were intelligent eyes. That was what he liked about them. In fact, her face was nice altogether. Straight, unremarkable nose, strong chin, prettily curved mouth, smooth skin.

It was difficult to tell about her figure, since she wore a rather bulky sweater and baggy jeans, yet it didn't matter. She was a pretty girl, there was no doubt in Hans's mind, but she clearly didn't know it.

Overall, though, she looked quite different from the women he dated, he thought idly. There was nothing ostentatious about her. Hers was a quiet, understated beauty that appealed to him on every level.

Her personality was another thing. She was more outspoken than he was used to, bolder. Very pleasant but there was a strength beneath the surface that gave him pause. After all, was an American—were all women raised in America so outspoken? The thought concerned him since he had just hired an American woman, sight unseen, to be the English teacher and caretaker for his two daughters.

Of course, the woman he'd hired—Anastasia Barimer—had impeccable references. There was considerable reassurance in that. She'd worked at the exclusive girls' school that his late wife and mother-in-law had attended—one of the most prestigious schools in America. In hiring her, he'd fulfilled his late wife's single wish for her daughters—that they wouldn't be packed off to boarding school thousands of miles from home as she had been. Though there had been a lot of distance between Hans and Marie, physically and emotionally, he had enough respect for her to comply with the simple wish she had had for their daughters' education.

Pendleton School for Girls had a lot of respect for Marie, too, and he knew they would never send someone unsuitable. Yes, he reassured himself, he'd done the right thing by hiring an American for his daughters.

And for the future of the monarchy. His people wanted to further international relations. He had several ideas of how to do so, but it would also be a good idea for his daughters to begin learning English from a native. They'd had some lessons, of course, from Frau Markham, but her knowledge of the language was limited. The new teacher would be able to teach them all of the nuances of the language, the idioms, the colloquialisms, all of the things they'd need to know as ambassadors for their country. Truthfully, he could use the practice himself. His plan was that they would only speak English in the house while the teacher was there.

He'd planned it completely and saw little to no room for error. He only hoped she wouldn't be as headstrong as this Annie seemed to be.

He also hoped she wouldn't be as young. And as…appealing.

Not that it mattered. He hadn't wanted Annie to stay and talk during the train ride because of her looks. He'd asked her because he thought she might have some interesting opinions on his country. The fact that this was her first time here made her an ideal person to get a fresh outlook on Kublenstein. That and the fact that she apparently didn't recognize him.

He'd spent the last week traveling alone—without bodyguards and secretaries—living among his people, in small villages and towns, and listening to their concerns about their country. The one thing that had come up over and over again was the fact that Kublenstein wasn't an international player. Most of the world hadn't even heard of Kublenstein, and those who had regarded it as a quaint little throwback vacation spot. But the people of Kublenstein wanted a voice in the European Economic Community. They wanted to be a force in exports and have the respect of the world for their watchmaking and their chocolates, in particular.

After hearing all of that, and agreeing with it, Hans could hardly pass up the opportunity to talk with an open-minded foreigner.

"What is it you do in America?" he asked her, telling himself that his interest was purely clinical and that he was, effectively, gathering data for his interview. Information like the curve of her mouth when she spoke or the brightness that seemed to emanate from behind her eyes would have to be dismissed as irrelevant.

She paused and her chest rose gently as she took a breath. "School librarian."

"Ah." He nodded. For some reason it surprised him, though he didn't know what he'd expected. "A librarian. So what made you decide to come to Kublenstein? Did the students at your school study it?"

She paused thoughtfully. "Well, some have heard the story about the little peasant girl who stopped the war for a day." Legend had it that a little girl had found a wounded enemy soldier on her front porch during a World War I battle and had assisted him despite the pleas from both sides to return to the safety of her home. While she was out there, no shots were fired.''

''That's just a myth.''

''Isn't there a statue built to her in the town square?'' Annie asked, reaching for her tour book.

''Yes, but the story is exaggerated.'' He was troubled. ''Is that all American students learn about Kublenstein?''

''Well…'' She didn't want to offend him, so she didn't point out that it was very few students who even knew that much. ''It's a very small country.''

That attitude always annoyed him, even though it was true. ''Smaller than some, yes, but bigger than others.''

''It's more of an underrated place than small, I think,'' Annie amended. ''The only time I can remember any mention of Kublenstein at all was in a history class, and that was just a passing reference that had something to do with Switzerland's neutrality. But I think it is a charming place.''

''Charming,'' he repeated, rolling the word out as if to decide whether he liked it or not.

She pressed her lips together then looked at him seriously. ''Oh, yes. Charm means a lot to me. I don't visit a place because of how far apart the borders are, I go for what's inside.''

He looked at her with interest. ''And what do you think you'll find inside Kublenstein?'' He'd only known her briefly, but he already knew enough to realize such a question could be dangerous when posed to such an honest young woman.

She gave a wry laugh. ''I really don't know. But

other places in Europe are bound to be loaded with tourists. Like Paris. I was just there and it was mobbed. But take a place like Lassberg, that you don't hear much about, and you probably can have the place to yourself.''

He kept his reaction under tight control. He knew she didn't mean to touch a nerve by pointing out the lack of tourists. "People do live here, you know.''

"Oh, I know. That's what's so exciting about it. You can visit and live among the people rather than a bunch of other tourists.'' She looked at him with a question in her eyes. "Wouldn't you rather keep the tourists out? I mean, as a native, wouldn't you rather preserve your country's natural charm than exploit it?''

He tightened his jaw and looked out the window. "Kublenstein, like every other European country, needs the revenues that tourism brings in. Without it, the charm you are so interested in would deteriorate.''

"Hmm. I hadn't thought of it that way.'' She looked out the window again. "It seems a shame.''

"It's the way it is,'' he said, under his breath. It wasn't her that he was upset with, but the truth of what she said.

"I hope I haven't offended you,'' she said.

She was obviously sincere. "No, of course you haven't. You were just being honest,'' he said magnanimously. Though the news of how little-known Kublenstein was in America wasn't good, she had told him something of what he needed to know about the American perception of his country.

"Anyway," she went on. "The size of a place doesn't make any difference when you consider that you're trapped in your own head no matter where you are. I mean, even now, in this compartment on the train, I'm stretching my wings more than I ever have in my life."

He couldn't help but feel caught up by her enthusiasm. "That's a good thing, yes?" For just a moment, he wished he could share the same feeling that she seemed to be experiencing.

She gave him a radiant smile, which made his chest tighten. "You know, as strange as it sounds, I feel great. Like something incredible is about to happen."

It was. He could see it in her eyes. For just a moment, he almost felt it, too, but the feeling was soon replaced by the crashing loneliness that was more familiar to him. Not self-pity, just the solitary existence he'd grown used to over the years.

"This is such beautiful countryside," she commented, bringing him out of his own thoughts.

He looked to see the familiar mountain peak where his palace was nestled. "Ah, yes," he said, gesturing toward the window. He was almost home. A small thrill of relief went through him, as it always did. "Although, as you pointed out, it's small."

She looked at him and he saw she understood his implication completely. "I didn't mean to touch a nerve."

He didn't like being read that easily. He pointed to the cathedral outside. "We're coming to the Lassberg city limits now. That's the Bonner Cathedral."

She followed the line of his hand. "It looks like something from Hans Christian Andersen. Everything here does. I keep thinking that."

He'd always taken great pride in the beauty of his country, and it pleased him no end to see the admiration in her eyes, despite what she'd said earlier. It had been a long time since he'd seen someone look at his land with the kind of awe he thought it deserved.

The fact that she did warmed his heart and his feelings toward her.

"No wonder so many fairy tales were written around here," she said wistfully, looking, for a moment, with such longing that he wondered what was in her heart. She answered the unasked question. "This looks just like the kind of land where people could live happily ever after."

He gave a brief nod. "Yes. Some people, I suppose." Foolish, romantic people.

She laughed and stretched her arms out over her head for a moment, saying, "I hope more than just some."

Expectation shone in her eyes. He spoke before he thought. "I'm quite certain you would, if you stayed," he reassured her, then stopped, startled by his own feelings. Why had he said that? How silly to be carried away by her ebullience that way.

She met his eyes, and for just an instant they shared some undefinable exchange.

"That is, I believe you'll like it here," he said, trying to regain his footing. He had to remain detached, had to command respect. It had been drilled into him since birth. So why did he slip now? It had to be exhaustion because he couldn't possibly feel as at ease with this woman as it seemed. "While you're here. Most of our few tourists enjoy their visit."

"I think I will," she agreed, then yawned. "Sorry. Anyway, I already am. Enjoying your country, I mean. And I caught that 'few tourists' crack."

He couldn't help but smile back. Intelligent girl. He'd known her for not more than an hour, and she'd already raised just about every emotion in him. He could not remember ever having met someone so simultaneously exasperating and fascinating.

If she was staying longer, he might want to get to know her better. Just to figure out what it was about her that had him so...piqued.

Thank goodness she wasn't staying.

"You know what's interesting?" Annie said, stopping his wandering thoughts. "You strike me as a very solitary person. It surprises me that you actually want more tourism in your country."

She'd pegged him. "My personal desires are not always commensurate with the needs of my country. When it comes to a choice between their needs versus my own, I have to honor my country over myself."

Her eyebrows shot up. "Wow, you're really patriotic."

"I have to be. It's my job."

Annie clicked her tongue. "I know plenty of civil servants who don't give a darn about anything but their paychecks."

"Their work must not be very fulfilling then."

"Is yours?" she asked, slicing right into the heart of the matter.

He considered her for a moment, then said, "I don't think I know you well enough to answer that question."

She looked a little bemused, but accepted his answer. "Okay. I don't want to pry." She didn't leave it at that, though. He'd known her only an hour or so, but he already knew her well enough to know that it would have gone against her character to leave it at that. "But if I were to guess," she went on, "I'd say it wasn't."

He looked at her. "Really."

"I mean, if it was, you'd probably be glad to say so. People usually refuse to share their negative feelings but not their positive ones."

He tried to remain impassive. "Interesting observation."

She yawned again. "Not that I know you well enough to tell, of course."

"No," he said evenly. "You don't." Yet somehow he felt she did, or could very easily.

She splayed her arms. "Feel free to correct me on anything I get wrong here."

He raised an eyebrow. "You sound like a journalist."

"Or maybe I'm psychic." She smiled, joking. "Does that frighten you?"

He waited, then answered honestly though with a slight smile. "More than you can imagine."

She must have dozed for just a minute without realizing it because Annie suddenly found herself leaning against the window with Hans reading a newspaper in front of her. How long had she been out?

Thank goodness he wasn't looking at her, because as she came around she had lingering daydream images of herself and Hans in unspeakable—but unforgettable—entanglements together. Yet the lingering feeling she had from the dreams was not of sexual fulfillment, but of emotional fulfillment. For just those brief few minutes that she had dreamed, Hans had been the answer to every ache and pain of loneliness that she'd ever felt.

Which was just how illogical dreams were, really, because while the man in front of her was the stuff of sexual dreams, he didn't seem to have a single impulse for fun. And though he'd been kind to offer to help her, he wasn't exactly a warm man.

But something in her said that he could be. That he needed someone to cover him and warm him and show him how to enjoy life and not just be all business all the time.

"Then again, you probably have a wife for that, don't you?" she said under her breath.

He lowered the newspaper and looked at her in a way that made her feel she'd made a terrible mistake.

She straightened in her seat and resisted the urge to clap a hand over her mouth. Had he really heard that? What was he, bionic?

"I'm sorry, what did you say?" he asked.

She stumbled over her response. "I—I—I was, um, saying that I suppose your wife," she searched frantically for something to say, "takes care of the children while you're away." It was a terrible improvisation, but it was too late to stop. "You did say you have children?"

He gave her a long look, then shook his head. "I didn't, no."

"Oh, my mistake then." The train began to slow as it entered the outskirts of Lassberg. She took the opportunity to begin gathering her things.

"I do, though."

"Do…?"

"Have children. But my wife died a few years ago."

She looked up, surprised. "I'm sorry to hear that."

He gave a small, unreadable, shrug.

"How old are your children?" she asked, careful not to tread on potentially painful territory.

A small light came into his dark eyes, like a match lit in a large dark room. "Very young. Both are under ten."

Like the de la Fuenza children she was going to care for. She loved elementary school age, an age when they began to be interested in books and in the outside world. "It must be difficult raising them on your own."

He splayed his arms. "I have a staff to help with that."

"A staff. My goodness, that sounds so—so large. Is that common in Kublenstein?"

He was thoughtful. "More so than in America, I think. Do you not have nannies and governesses in America?"

"It's very rare."

"Then who cares for the children when both parents work or are unavailable?"

"Well, there's day care, school. People work it out, though it's not always very easy. I think it's something of a luxury to be able to stay home with them or have someone else stay home with them."

"Mmm." He nodded. "I'm very interested in the American way of raising children. Some aspects, anyway," he amended. "For example, American children tend to be so confident. Bold. Those are good qualities."

"Absolutely. After working in a school for so long, I've seen a pretty direct link between high self-esteem and lots of family involvement."

He shifted in his seat. "Really? In what way do you mean that, family involvement?"

She stepped carefully, conscious not to insult him. "I just mean when parents spend as much time as they can with their children, the children benefit." And Annie knew from her own experience the damage that could be done when there was no one around to take an interest in a child's life.

"Often it's not possible to spend a lot of time with the children."

She shrugged. "So you make time."

He looked out the window for a moment.

"Still, you're a single father," Annie went on. "That can't be easy."

"No," he agreed. "There are times when it can be trying. They need a woman's influence more than they need mine. They've had many caretakers yet at times they still seem so…needy. So emotional.''

''Well, there's your problem right there,'' Annie said, without stopping to think about whether she should or not.

A wall went up behind his eyes. ''I beg your pardon?''

She realized her mistake immediately. ''Nothing,'' she said, trying to backpedal. ''I shouldn't have said anything. It's none of my business.''

He hesitated. He was inclined to agree with her. But seeing as how he'd only be with her for a few more minutes before they parted and he would never see her again, he felt he could listen to her opinions a bit more. After all, he'd just hired an American. It was important for him to know what kind of style he might be dealing with. ''No, no, please go on. I asked you. I truly am interested in the American perspective.''

''Well…'' She shrugged again. ''You said you'd hired 'many caretakers' but what kids really need is one person they can depend on. Preferably you, since you're…around…'' She paused just for an instant. ''There is an emotional risk to them if you hire a rapid succession of caretakers.''

He was genuinely puzzled. ''Emotional risk?''

She frowned. ''Yes. In not having one single caretaker to rely on, whether it's you or someone you hire. But preferably you.''

His defenses went up. He wanted her general opinion, not a personal judgment. ''The children know they can rely on whomever I choose to hire.''

"But maybe that's not enough."

"It's enough," he said shortly.

A vague protectiveness for the unknown children rose in Annie's heart. "All right," she conceded. "Just let me say this. Children need to have people in their lives who will be there for them, even when you think it's not important, like after school, before bed, whatever. They need to know that they can count on that person to be there, to be available if they need them. Not just *a* person, but someone they love and trust, and who loves them, too." Annie knew she might be overstepping the bounds of courtesy, but the conversation struck too close to her heart for her to be concerned about being polite.

He nodded slowly, watching her. Then a tiny smile nudged at the corner of his sensuous mouth. "You don't have children of your own, do you?"

"As I said, I've worked with children for years."

"Yes, well, until you have them, perhaps you don't realize exactly what their needs are."

"Maybe you're right." Her voice was quiet, but hard.

Satisfied that the conversation was settled, Hans leaned back and began thinking about the list of things he had to take care of that afternoon. He was very anxious to get away from this conversation.

"In general," she said, cutting into the silence, "if a person has been through a long line of caretakers and can't understand why the children are emotionally needy, I don't think that person has been listening to them."

Hans shifted in his seat and looked at her, hard. "May I ask why you feel so strongly about this?"

Her face went scarlet.

"It's personal, isn't it?" Hans went on. "This isn't some general theory of child rearing, it's a very specific—how do you say it?—pet peeve of yours."

After a long hesitation, she said, "I guess you could say that. But it doesn't change the truth of the matter."

"What is your reason?" And why did he want, so much, to know what had hurt her in the past? His curiosity about this woman was inexplicable.

She shook her head and waved the question away. "It's boring. Forget it, I shouldn't have been so outspoken with you."

He looked at her for a moment, then shifted his eyes to the window behind her, searching for a way to change the subject from a topic that was clearly a very emotional one to this young woman. "The train has stopped. We're at the station."

She looked and saw they were, indeed, stopped in the station and people had already begun to disembark.

"I hope you understand that I meant no personal offense," she offered, for the second time in an hour.

"I asked your opinion and you gave it."

They stood simultaneously and their hands bumped against one another. Annie felt a palpable heat generate between them, but now she wasn't sure if it was attraction or frustration.

"Well, it's been an interesting trip," she said, trying to break the ice before they went their separate ways.

He cocked his head. "Interesting, indeed." He held out his hand.

Believing he intended to shake hands, she put hers out but he raised it to his lips. As he did so, she felt a shock of pleasure run up her arm and into her heart. He must have felt something, too, because he snapped back and met her eyes.

"It was a pleasure to meet you," he said, composing himself quickly. They walked out of the compartment and down the hall to the train exit. Hans put his arm around Annie to help her off the train, then quickly dropped it to his side.

A small group of women several feet away began to murmur among themselves, and Hans grew even more uncomfortable. A large cab headed in their direction, and Hans held a hand up for it. The driver pulled over and Hans leaned into the window and said something in rapid German to him. He then opened the door for Annie.

"Enjoy your stay in Kublenstein," he said, giving her a lingering look. He began to say something else, then stopped.

"Thanks," she said, climbing into the cab. "I will."

"Goodbye," he said, shutting the door. He turned to walk away from her.

"Goodbye," she said softly inside the empty cab. She watched him walk away.

When he was out of sight she wondered why she suddenly felt so empty.

Chapter Three

The hotel her new employer had suggested for Annie was exquisite. Decorated with antiques and overlooking the charming street below, it was the most comfortable room Annie had stayed in since arriving in Europe. It was also about half the price of the overpriced modest room with plastic cube furniture she'd rented in Munich.

She sat in a wingback chair by the window and thought about the upcoming year. Watching the people on the street—apple-cheeked women carrying paper bags of bread and produce, children running behind them in what looked more like homemade clothes than the designer wear the students at Pendleton preferred—Annie thought she could stay in Lassberg forever. Until today, she hadn't realized such a place still existed in the world.

What was it going to be like to stay? she wondered. Would she make friends outside of the household? Could she have a social life somehow?

Would she ever see Hans again?

She tried to squelch the thought. After all, she knew he lived in this small city. How could they not run into each other at some point?

And if they did, what would she say?

Hans, hello, I hope you weren't upset by my evil twin on the train. Sometimes she speaks out of turn.

But she hadn't spoken out of turn, she felt strongly about everything she'd said.

Perhaps she would just pretend there had been no acrimony.

Hans! How great to see you again! Would you like to go for a cup of coffee?

Or would that be too forward?

Finally she decided that if she saw him again, she would probably melt at his feet and not have to worry about what to say at all. He could speak first. She was much better at responding than at improvising the first words.

Across the square a steeple clock began to ring the hour. Five o'clock. As if on cue, small flurries of snow began to drift down from the clouds. Annie watched in amazement, her heart full. It felt like a miracle, and she wished there was someone to share it with. Green eyes came to mind, and gleaming dark hair, but she pushed the thought of the man away.

She watched, and dreamed, for perhaps fifteen minutes. The street had a thin veil of white over it. Finally she stood up and stretched. It was time to eat. Incredibly, the meal was included with the price of the room. As she'd gotten into the cage elevator she could have sworn she smelled Swiss Cheese Fondue. Her mouth watered just thinking about it.

She went to her suitcase and took out a sweater and some warm pants. Perhaps she'd walk through the town after dinner, and try to acquaint herself with the layout.

The meal was, indeed, a rich fondue. The cook had made fresh bread minutes before Annie had gone to eat, and the yeasty-cheesy scent in the dining room was as warming as an eiderdown comforter. She ate hungrily, devouring the faintly nutty-flavored Gruyère cheese fondue, the crisp green salad, and not one but two cups of warm chocolate pudding. The cook had been delighted to see her eating so heartily.

Afterwards, she took a long, leisurely walk through the town. It was even lovelier than she'd thought, with several wooden toy shops, a clock maker, a lively corner pub where people were playing darts, and several other Dickensian-looking shops. She imagined herself taking this walk every night after dinner. Then she imagined herself at dinner with Hans across the table. Better still, she imagined sitting on the woolen rug in front of the fire with Hans…or lying on the rug in front of the fire with Hans… The thought raised gooseflesh on her arms.

She got back to her room at eight o'clock and was asleep by eight-fifteen. She slept deeply and woke ten hours later, at 6:00 a.m. Kublenstein-time. It was still dark outside, but the snow had covered everything, bringing a faint white glow to the land.

She felt both inspired and achingly lonely. After calculating the time in Maryland, she decided to call Joy. She could always make Annie feel grounded again. She took her phone card out of her duffel bag and called.

"Have you met him?" Joy asked, as soon as she heard Annie's voice.

"Who?" Annie asked, though now, unbeknownst to Joy, she knew the answer.

"Anyone?"

Annie smiled to herself, thinking for a moment about keeping Hans a secret for herself. She couldn't, though. "Yes, there was a man on the train, but I don't even know his last name. I don't think I'll see him again."

"Was he attractive?"

"Unbelievably."

"And you let him get away?"

She smiled a little sadly. "As a matter of fact, that's just what it was like. He was fairly eager to get away from me by the time we got to the city."

"What did you do?"

"Basically told him his country was small and insignificant, though charming, and that he was raising his children wrong."

"Bad move."

"You're telling me."

"Well, forget him then. I saw a clip of that Prince Johann guy on some show on royalty last night, and *he's* the one to go for. He's gorgeous."

"Come on, he's got to be, what, in his seventies?"

"Honey, if he's seventy, I'm eighty-five."

"Okay, Grandma. Look, I can't stay on long, I just wanted to hear a friendly voice."

"Homesick?" Joy asked knowingly. "Don't forget you can always come back home."

"I know it," Annie said, but as she spoke the words, she felt certain that she was home. She couldn't say that to Joy, though. She would never understand.

In fact, Annie could barely understand it herself.

On her third morning in Lassberg, Annie's sleep was interrupted by a knock at the door.

Annie put a robe on and opened the door a crack. When she saw it was the proprietress, she opened the door to let her in.

"There is a man waiting downstairs," the proprietress said in German. "He says he works for your new employer and that he's here to pick you up."

Annie rubbed her eyes and tried to make sense of it. "But that's crazy, they're not supposed to come until eleven." She looked at her watch and jumped. "Oh, my gosh, it's almost eleven now."

"What do you want me to do?" the woman asked, immediately flustered.

Annie quickly glanced around the room. "Stall him. I'll be down in ten minutes at the most." Annie said a small prayer of thanks that she had already packed all of her things and had taken a shower last night.

"You don't want to keep this man waiting," the landlady replied with a frown. "He's come in a very important car."

Annie tried to make sense of what the landlady meant, then realized the woman must be referring to her employer's government job. He had probably sent a diplomatic car or something. "Okay, I'll be down in a minute," she said.

It was only about eight minutes later when Annie came into the lobby. A small man, in an official-looking uniform, sat in the wingback chair in the corner of the lobby.

He stood when he saw her. "Miss Barimer?"

"Yes."

He gave a slight bow. "I'm Christian. I'll be driving you today." He nodded to her suitcases. "Is that all of your luggage?"

"That's it," she said.

Both women stood back as Christian signaled for two other men to collect the luggage and take it out to the car.

"I've taken care of the bill, so if you're ready, we can depart immediately."

With a quick goodbye to the proprietress, Annie followed Christian out to a long, silver Mercedes with the royal flags of Kublenstein and Lassberg on it.

"My gosh," she breathed. "What does Mr. de la Fuenza do for the government?"

"There is no Mr. de la Fuenza."

She froze halfway into the car. "What? I thought my employers were Mr. and Mrs. de la Fuenza."

Christian's face remained still, and he didn't answer.

Instead, the answer came from another man, a man

with an American accent, who was already waiting in the back seat of the limousine. "Marie de la Fuenza, died several years ago," he said as she climbed in next to him. "Your new employer is her husband, Prince Johann of Kublenstein."

There was no point in trying to imagine how she would have thought she'd react in this kind of situation because there was no way in the world Annie would ever have even dreamed she was going to be working for the prince.

"Who are you?" she asked the American man, trying to catch her breath.

"Forgive the cloak and dagger routine," he answered, with a nod of his gray head and a smile as cheery as Santa's. He held out a chubby hand. "Ben Lyman, I'm the American ambassador to Kublenstein. The prince and the late princess are old friends of mine, and it was I who suggested keeping his identity anonymous until you got here. It was for your protection as much as his and the children's, you understand."

She swallowed, trying to take it all in. "Okay." But she didn't quite understand. None of this made sense. Here she was, sitting in the back of a car more luxurious than her living room, watching the picturesque cuckoo-clock town fade away behind the car as it wound its way through a black forest, and up a magical-looking alpine road to the prince's palace.

As incredible as the situation was, it wasn't what she'd expected, and that was disconcerting.

Ben Lyman went on chatting about the background of the royal family and the history of the city as they drove along, but Annie could barely take it in. She was going to work for Prince Johann. That meant she was going to live in a palace of some sort for the next year. It was incredible.

Yet it was also daunting. She had to take the responsibility very, very seriously. There was no room for mistakes when taking care of any children, but especially not when taking care of future monarchs.

By the time the car drew into the brick courtyard in front of the enormous palace, Annie had come back down to earth. This was no dream. It was the nineteenth century come alive before her very eyes and she had an important role before her. It was more than disconcerting, it was almost frightening.

Ben walked Annie into the palace. She had the feeling from the looks of the staff members that they had expected someone grander, and probably older, than Annie.

Just as she was beginning to feel like her best move would be to turn and run, an elderly woman with a bright white smile came up to them. "You must be Anastasia Barimer," she said. "I'm Greta Entemain, the prince's personal secretary. Welcome."

"Thanks. You can call me Annie." She was so grateful for the woman's warmth that she nearly wept. "How do you do?" She extended her hand.

Greta took it and squeezed reassuringly. "Very well, thank you. Come right this way, his highness will be available to meet you in about twenty minutes." She patted Annie's forearm. "Follow me.

We'll get you a nice warm cup of chocolate and you can relax before speaking with his highness.''

His highness. The words sent a shiver of excitement down Annie's spine. This was going to be a very formal process, from beginning to end. She'd seen enough royal pomp and circumstance in the British royal weddings in the eighties to know Europeans took their traditions seriously.

She followed Greta down a long marble hall. The ceilings soared above them, perhaps as tall as three stories. The walls were ornately carved, occasionally punctuated by a beautiful oil painting or handmade tapestry. They seemed to walk a mile before finally turning into a large, bright kitchen.

One whole wall was lined with windows and sunlight gleamed off the chrome refrigerators and industrial-size stoves.

"Margaret Livens, this is Annie Barimer," Greta said, gesturing toward a small, heavyset woman with dark hair and small, laughing eyes. "Margaret is our cook."

"Nice to meet you," Annie said, looking around at the massive stoves and oven. "It looks like you have to do quite a lot of cooking."

"Quite a lot." Margaret nodded enthusiastically. Annie was surprised to note that she had a British accent. "Good thing I like to cook so much or I'd be crazy by now."

Greta touched Annie's arm. "If there's nothing else I can do to make you more comfortable, I'll excuse myself now. I'll come for you when his highness is ready to see you. Will you be comfortable here or should I show you to the library?''

"This is fine, really.''

"Very good.'' With a brief smile, Greta turned and left the room.

As soon as she was gone, Margaret brought a tray with two steaming mugs of hot chocolate to the table and sat down with Annie. "So.'' She poured cream from a small pitcher into one of the mugs, stirred the swirl in to make a pale chocolate, and handed it to Annie. "You here to take the governess and English teaching job, then?''

Annie took the warm mug and nodded. "That's right.'' She took a sip of the decadent creamy chocolate.

"You nervous?'' She didn't wait for an answer. "Myself, I was as nervous as a cat the first time I came here. You could have played guitar on my nerves, they were strung so tight.''

"How long did it take you to get over that?''

Margaret made a show of looking at her watch. "It's been two years so far...'' She laughed.

Annie took another taste of the chocolate. The sweetness warmed and soothed her. "I hope it doesn't take me that long,'' she said.

Margaret poured more cream into her chocolate. "You don't need to worry too much. Most of the nannies and teachers and governesses who come here don't stay that long anyway.''

"How many have there been?'' Annie asked. Another shoe was about to drop, and she had a feeling it was a cleat.

This was enough to make Margaret set down her mug, the sugar, and the cream. "What, didn't they tell you?"

Trepidation crept across Annie's skin. "Tell me what?"

Margaret shrugged. "By my count, there've been fifteen women through here this year alone."

"Fifteen!" Annie gasped. "What on earth is wrong with the children?"

"It's not the children," Margaret said, then lowered her voice and leaned in and whispered so low that Annie could barely hear her. "It's because of him."

Annie was half-ready to turn in her resignation as Greta led her into the prince's office. After all, why go into a miserable experience if you can do something about it in advance?

The marble hallway through the back of the palace was long and chilly. It gave Annie goose bumps, as if the centuries had brought change but had also held on to some ghosts. The ornaments that decorated the walls were fabulously extravagant, creating an atmosphere that she wasn't entirely comfortable with.

Their footsteps echoed like hushed voices as she and Greta swished through the ghosts of the past toward the prince's office. What was he like? Annie wondered. He probably fit into this atmosphere. People's surroundings usually did reflect themselves, though she wasn't so sure that was true in the case of a centuries-old royal household.

What would he look like? Was he like a cartoon

version of Prince Charming's father? No, that was too jolly. And Joy had said he was gorgeous, though Annie hadn't always agreed with her taste in men. Still, it probably meant that he wasn't in his nineties or anything. Was he more like a Paul Newman-ish kind of mature? Could the tyrant Margaret had described really look like that?

They stopped at a carved wooden door at the end of the hall and Greta gave a single knock. There was a muffled acknowledgement from the other side, so she opened the door and said, with a slight curtsy, "Your Highness, here is the new English teacher and governess for the children."

Annie took a deep breath and stepped over the threshold, wondering if she was expected to curtsy as well or if that would be presumptuous of her. She decided to compromise by bowing her head.

"Anastasia Barimer," Greta said, gesturing toward Annie. "Anastasia, this is your new employer, Crown Prince Johann of Kublenstein."

"How do you do?" Annie began, but when she saw who she was speaking to, she nearly dropped to the floor in a dead faint.

Hans, the good-looking civil servant from the train, surprise etched in his features, was behind the ornate desk.

"You," he said, in a soft tone. He immediately followed by straightening his back and clearing his throat. "I had no idea."

"Neither did I."

An extremely awkward moment passed.

"Take a seat, please," he told her, after a moment, gesturing to the chair before his desk in the same way he'd indicated the seat on the train three days before.

And as she'd done then, she sat before him. As the initial shock of adrenaline faded, she began to feel a growing sense of inevitability. A kind of understanding. Somehow the pieces were falling into place. He'd spoken of losing his wife, of having been through a series of caretakers for his daughters, of having a large household to maintain.

"I...I apologize for the secrecy with which we had to arrange for your arrival," he began. "I hope you can understand my reticence to divulge all before arranging for you to come here."

"Absolutely." She steadied herself and tried to return her thoughts to the job instead of the figure he cut, but it was difficult. He was a *prince,* for crying out loud. A real prince. She felt a sigh build in her chest. He was so handsome it was almost impossible to comprehend. How was it that such a gorgeous man reigned in such a lovely European country and she'd never even heard about him? It seemed the world-wide press limited their coverage to the British royal family.

Every once in awhile she'd heard of Princess or Prince so-and-so of a country she hadn't realized even had a monarchy, but she'd never thought any of the European monarchs were so young and attractive. She'd always pictured them as movie characters, either elderly and kind or young and goofy.

Hans was definitely neither of those.

"We have to be very careful when hiring new staff," he continued.

She nodded. It wasn't easy to regain her composure. "I—I'd imagine there are a lot of people who would love to work with the royal children but who wouldn't even stop to help an ordinary child cross the street."

He grimaced and gave a short nod. "I'm afraid that's true. It's been very difficult to find someone suitable. I hope we've done so now." But Annie thought he looked skeptical.

Very skeptical.

Hans couldn't hide his amazement that the woman he'd hired from a prestigious boarding school five thousand miles away, with the best references possible and a personal profile fit for a royal household, could be the same woman who had exasperated him to the point of distraction on the train. For one thing, she was far too young to take responsibility for the young princesses. More to the point, she was headstrong, opinionated, outspoken, and perhaps even a little brash.

He hadn't been able to get her off his mind.

Granted, he'd asked for her opinion—and God knew he'd gotten it—but that was before he'd known he would have to deal with her again. He'd already let down the reserve that should exist between employer and employee. She knew him as Hans, even, not by his proper title. It would be twice as hard to establish a proper business relationship now.

Suddenly aware that Greta was still in the room,

and quite possibly reading his thoughts, he said, "That will be all, thank you, Greta."

"Very well, sir." With a puzzled look at the two of them, she left the room.

"In company," he said, when Greta had left the room, "you will address me as Prince Johann."

"Of course." Annie looked around. "Are we in company now?"

"No," he said slowly. This was trouble. Every nerve in his body told him so. "Now we are alone."

She frowned. "Then what do I call you now?"

He looked back at Annie. "In private, you may call me 'sir.'"

"Prince Johann in public, 'sir' in private. Got it."

"Except when there is a state function in the palace and you are present, then you address me with my title, Your Royal Highness." He glanced at his watch, frowned, and rubbed his thumb across a smudge on the crystal.

Annoyance niggled at her. "And what will you call me?"

He shifted his gaze from his watch to her eyes. "I beg your pardon?"

She took a breath, then asked, "What will you call me when we're at a state function in the palace and when we're in private?"

"I will call you Miss Barimer."

"All the time?" If this was the real Hans, she wasn't sure she liked him. What had happened to the man on the train who had listened instead of giving orders?

He hesitated for one interminable moment, scrutinizing her to try and determine if she was deliberately baiting him. "Except when something else seems more appropriate."

"I see." She raised her chin. "Do I have the same option?"

He took her meaning immediately and was surprised at his impulse to laugh. "There are those who might say you're being impertinent."

"That's true." He had only one comfortable moment before she went on to say, "If you'll forgive me, there are those who might say you're being arrogant."

This was no withering flower who would do what he asked the way the rest of his staff did. She was trouble, he'd known it from the moment he'd met her. It was just that then he hadn't realized she was his trouble. "Arrogant?" he repeated.

She nodded. "Why 'sir' now and 'Hans' on the train?" she asked defiantly.

"Because on the train you were not my employee."

"I was. You just didn't realize it yet. Neither did I, of course."

"Miss Barimer, it might be wise to avoid the issue of our conversation on the train. We will probably both be better off if we start over."

"But," she paused, "sir, I meant what I said on the train." There was a subtle, stubborn set to her feminine jaw that warned him that she wasn't joking. He remembered that look—along with the fiery flashes in her pale eyes—from the train, as she'd talked about how children needed stability and love.

Perhaps that was good. He wanted someone who cared passionately, though he didn't necessarily agree with her assessment of his own situation.

"All right. On the train you spoke of stability, which I can assure you my children have."

"It didn't sound like it," she ventured, with a shake of her head.

"I consider the constant attention to their education, clothing, and physical well-being, not to mention their homes in the city and the country, to be plenty of stability. Additionally, there are plenty of staff members who have been in the household since before the girls were born, who have known them and cared about them all of their lives." It was true. Greta had been his secretary for at least ten years now. Leo had been his chief advisor for closer to twenty, though Leo, with his chilly, stiff demeanor, probably wasn't the kind of stable figure Annie had in mind. Then there was Christian, who was Hans's driver and had been Hans's father's driver before that.

"'Cared about them'?" she repeated. "That's all well and good, but what about love?"

What a typically American attitude. He found himself smiling. It was really quite quaint the way she prioritized emotion. Naturally he loved his children more than anything, but he wasn't sure where that belonged on the hierarchy of needs for the young princesses. Discipline was also extremely important for royal children. So were manners and etiquette, dignity inside the palace walls and outside. He regarded Annie with a skeptical eye. "Miss Barimer,

I asked you once why you feel so strongly about this that you're willing to fight it. At the time you said it wasn't worth talking about. But now the matter seems to be relevant to your employment here, so I wish you would be more direct about your concerns.''

She swallowed. ''You don't want to hear about my personal history.''

''I do.''

She took a wavering breath and appeared to think carefully, as if trying to sort which details she'd give and which she wouldn't. ''I grew up with a very strong sense of family and security. My mother and father were always there for me as a child, always willing to lend an ear when I was troubled, or give a few minutes' time when I needed help with homework.'' Her voice grew tight and she took a moment before continuing. ''It made all the difference in my life.'' She shrugged helplessly. ''When I hear about children who don't have that kind of nurturing and care, it makes me very sad.''

Hans suspected there was more to the story than she had mentioned, but he didn't want to push her. Even now he was gripped by a ridiculous urge to reach out to her and comfort her in his arms. Instead he cleared his throat and straightened his sleeves. ''I see. Well, thank you for telling me about that. I understand better why you feel strongly about this issue. However, I do hope you'll be able to acknowledge that there are other ways for families to interact and one is not necessarily better than the other.'' He didn't wait for an answer. "Now. How much do you know about protocol?"

She looked thrown by his question for a moment, then raised her chin and said, "Not a thing, sir."

"Then you'll have to learn. Greta can help with that. One of your duties will be to help teach the girls how to be gracious and correct in their public roles."

After just a moment's hesitation, she nodded. "I understand."

That encouraged him. Perhaps she could be persuaded to do the duties he expected of her, stubborn and modern as she was. Clearly she had been well-bred, although she had perhaps been given too much of a free rein. She'd come from a good family, according to his research and according to what she, herself, had just said. And as a multilingual representative of Pendleton, she had also been to numerous embassy events in nearby Washington, D.C., where many of the students' parents lived. And truth be told, he appreciated that her approach to the children was warmer than his wife's—or even his mother's—had been.

He realized he was talking himself into her, and wondered why, since at this point he didn't have much choice. He'd hired her already and brought her over from the United States. He had to at least give her a try.

If she didn't work out, he could always let her go.

Hans decided to ignore the feeling of despair that overcame him when he thought about letting Annie leave.

Chapter Four

When her talk with Hans—Prince Johann—was finished, Greta showed Annie to her new room. The place that would be home for the next year.

"Where are the children?" Annie asked, awkwardly adjusting her grip on one of her suitcases, which were getting heavier with every step, as she straggled behind Greta.

"The children are in their room. You'll meet them presently." She turned and cast an affectionately critical eye on Annie. "You really ought to have let someone carry your bags for you."

"I had no idea it would be such a long walk. This place must be as big as Versailles." Annie smiled, wondering what Hans's reaction would be to her bringing up the size of his domain once again.

"Here we are." Greta stopped in front of a white, carved wooden door, one of at least twenty just like

it in the hall. She took the brass knob in hand and
opened the door with a flourish, announcing, "Your
quarters."

Annie glanced quickly behind her to try and count
doors so she could find her way back on her own,
but there were too many. And she hadn't brought
bread crumbs. With a sigh she turned back and
walked over the threshold. As soon as she did, she
caught her breath.

Greta smiled.

Annie glanced at her, then back at the room. The
grandeur was breathtaking. The walls, which were at
least twenty feet tall, were papered in a delicate rose-
and-gold-striped pattern. It framed, beautifully, a
large bay window which looked out over the mountainside. The ceilings soared overhead, with ornate
crown moldings in gleaming gold. The bed was extra
wide and stood high off the ground, with a wooden
step on the side, and a fancy canopy that arched overhead. It was a Victorian vision of grace and feminin-
ity. Annie felt as though she'd stepped through the
looking glass into her own private Wonderland.

"There's the wardrobe, and the door to the nursery
is just there," Greta was saying, busily waving her
arm about to indicate things that should be of interest
to Annie. "And this—"

"Pardon me."

Annie and Greta both started at the low voice that
interrupted them. When Greta turned to the doorway,
her eyes grew wide. Annie followed her gaze to
Hans. Her first thought was to wonder why Greta
looked so surprised to see him.

"That will be all, thank you, Greta." A quick nod of his head left no doubt that she was excused.

"Yes, sir." Greta cast a quick glance from him to Annie before leaving the room.

She left a thick silence behind her.

"You seem to have the most astounding way of making people scurry around you," Annie said lightly.

"You don't scurry, I notice," he answered evenly, but she thought she detected a hint of a smile in his eyes.

"Was I meant to?"

This time he did smile, causing Annie to catch her breath inside. "You've had several opportunities." He crossed the room at a leisurely pace and stopped by the window. "Not least of which was when you discovered I was to be your employer here in Lassberg," he said, without turning around so she could tell whether he was glad she'd stayed.

"Did you want me to?" she asked.

He turned back, then, his level gaze inscrutable. "It would not have surprised me at all if that had been your impulse."

She had felt a lot of things when she'd seen Hans sitting behind that big desk, and running was certainly one of them. The most overwhelming sense she'd had, though, was shock, then curiosity and a sense of relief that she was able to see him one more time. She wanted to see what happened next, how this could possibly turn out. "I am committed to the position of taking care of your children," she said, trying to maintain a professional air. "I wouldn't run away from that responsibility. Or the opportunity, for that matter.''

Their eyes met for a shivering moment, then he moved across the room in great strides. ''I'm very glad to hear it.''

''I'm very excited about this job,'' she went on. ''Despite our, um, rather unusual introduction, I think we'll work very well together.''

Something in him bristled. ''Not together, precisely, but I take your meaning.''

She flushed. ''Right.''

There was a brief silence.

Annie filled it. ''Between the two of us, the children should have a nice balance of influences.''

''I'm glad.''

''Look, Hans—I mean, sir—I really hope you won't hold our conversation on the train against me. I would never have addressed you so informally if I'd known who you were.''

''Perhaps it was best that you didn't know who I was, then. I don't want you to be other than yourself with me, Miss Barimer, or with the children.''

''Oh, no, of course not. They can see right through that.'' She looked like she was finished speaking, then suddenly she caught her breath. ''Not that you couldn't see through it, if someone were to…'' Lost, she shrugged helplessly.

He narrowed his eyes, scrutinizing her.

She cleared her throat. ''I'm dying to meet the children. Greta said their room adjoins this one?''

''Yes. Yes it does.'' Looking relieved to have an interruption, he went to a door on the wall opposite and opened it. "Besa, Marta, come here please," he called into the next room.

Down the hall there was a loud crash. Annie started, but Hans just frowned. "That infernal maid has broken three lamps this week. A broken engagement is no reason for—"

"Yes, Father?"

Two young girls had appeared in the doorway, making the question of the maid's broken engagement and Hans's insensitivity to it disappear in Annie's mind.

Both the girls had hair so pale it looked almost white, and both wore pale blue gingham pinafores. They looked like something out of an old children's book, in dresses which, while cute in an old-fashioned way, would have been wholly impractical for playing outdoors.

"Yes, Father?" they both said in German.

He answered in the same language. "This is your new governess, Miss Barimer." He gestured broadly toward Annie. "She will be helping you with English, among other things. From now on, that is the language we'll speak in her presence."

"Yes, Father."

"We will, Father."

He looked pleased. "Miss Barimer, this is Marta." He put a hand on the shoulder of the taller girl. Annie noted that she had the deep green eyes of her father.

"How do you do, ma'am?" Marta curtsied.

"Call me Annie," Annie said with a warm smile.

"They'll call you Miss Barimer," Hans said shortly.

She looked at him, surprised. "Very well, if that's what you prefer."

"It is." He raised an eyebrow. Clearly he wanted no challenge. "They must treat their elders with respect. This is not summer camp."

"I understand." Stung, she turned her attention to the other child and tried to smile again, but it was difficult with Hans's dark gaze scrutinizing her. She felt like he was ready to pounce at any moment. She crouched down in front of the younger child and said, "You must be Besa, then."

Besa had pale, pale blue eyes, and doll-like dimples when she smiled. "Yes, ma'am."

Annie took a deep breath. These children would be a pleasure to work with, she could tell that already. If only she could say the same for her employer. She stood up and looked Hans evenly in the eye. She was not going to be intimidated by him, no matter how hard he tried. "I think we're going to get along beautifully, the children and I."

"I'm counting on it." He patted the girls on their heads. "All right, be good girls, mind Miss Barimer." To Annie, he added, "You and the children will be dining at 7:00 p.m. in the main dining hall."

She didn't know where that was, but she decided quickly that she'd rather roam the palace for half an hour looking than ask him for directions. "Okay. We'll see you there."

The princesses looked at each other.

"Father doesn't dine with us," Marta said, in a tone that verged on condescending. She must have learned it from her father, Annie concluded, as she clearly wasn't doing it on purpose.

"He doesn't?"

"Oh, no, he dines after we've gone to bed."

"After you've gone to bed?" Annie looked at Hans questioningly.

He raised an eyebrow at the expression on her face. "I trust this is not a problem for you, Miss Barimer." He turned to leave.

"Sir," Annie began.

Hans stopped and turned around, looking impatient. "What is it?"

She glanced at the girls, then said, "May I have a quick word with you in the hall?"

He gave a short sigh. "Children, go back to your room. Miss Barimer will join you there in a moment."

The girls nodded and went back through the door they'd come in.

"What did you want to discuss?" Hans asked when they were gone.

Annie carefully closed the door behind the children and turned back to Hans. "Well, when we met you specifically mentioned an interest in how Americans raise children. That's the only reason I mention this, believe me—"

"Yes, yes, what is the problem?"

Her face warmed, but she went on. "Well, in America families eat together."

"That is not how we do it here."

"I understand that, but since you expressed an interest in the way things are done in America, this would be one thing that would be easy to change and it could have a positive impact on the children. Perhaps you're not aware of them, but studies have been done in the United States that show children who eat dinner with their family every night are much more well adjusted than children who don't. Their grades are better, they don't tend to experiment with drugs—''

''We are not in the United States, Miss Barimer.'' The expression in his eyes warned that she was treading on dangerous terrain. ''My plan was that the girls would have some American influence, not that I, myself, would.''

''Yes, but—'' She stopped and obviously squelched whatever she'd been about to say. ''Okay.''

He should have walked away. He'd gained the position he needed in this relationship and leaving now would only strengthen it. He sighed. ''But what, Miss Barimer? What were you going to say?''

She clicked her tongue against her teeth. ''Only that I'm going to have to get used to trying to figure out when you want my influence and when you don't.''

There was a long pause, during which she could see he was formulating a patient but firm response. ''I'll do my best to be clear with you,'' he said, dismissing the subject.

Annie softened somewhat. ''Please believe me, I don't want to cause trouble by arguing about everything. I want to do a good job, to help these children,'' she was struck, suddenly, by the loneliness she perceived in his handsome visage. "I want to help *you*."

He stared at her for a moment, surprised at her silly, romantic plea. She was so naive about some things. It was charming…and exasperating. But what did he expect? She was so young. Or was she? A small smile came across his lips. "I appreciate the thought, Miss Barimer," he said softly. "But I am beyond your help." He turned to the door and opened it, then stopped and turned back to Annie. "I'll see you at seven o'clock in the main dining room."

She felt her heart expand like a balloon. "Oh, I'm so glad. You won't be sorry, honestly—"

"At seven, then," he interrupted sharply. The warmth was gone from his eyes, but it had been there for one brief moment. She'd seen it. "Don't be late."

Annie was late, of course. It wasn't on purpose, though. She'd actually left her room a couple of minutes earlier than she thought she needed to, so as to allow time to find the dining room. If she'd been taking care of the children, they could have shown her the way, but her duties didn't officially begin until the next day. The first day was for her to get settled in and learn her way around. After fumbling around the palace for twenty minutes before she found the dining room, she did feel she'd learned her way around.

She entered the dining room somewhat breathlessly, a fact that was accented by the silence in the room.

"I'm so sorry," she said, hurrying to the empty chair opposite Hans at the end of the table. "I had some…trouble." She didn't want to admit she'd been lost. "It won't happen again."

"Perhaps we should have maps made?" Hans said, with an eyebrow lifted.

"I'm sure I don't know what you mean," she said pointedly, but she couldn't help smiling.

"Father said he believed he heard your footsteps tapping back and forth overhead in the halls," Besa supplied eagerly. Her smile was bright. "He said if you didn't arrive soon, someone would have to go rent you."

"Rescue," Marta corrected, then turned to Annie. "He said someone would have to go rescue you."

"I see. Did he say who?" Annie asked, with a sidelong glance at Hans.

"It would have been my pleasure," he answered, and she knew he was laughing at her, but not in an unkind way.

"These walls and floors are too thick to hear footsteps through," Annie said.

"Nevertheless…" He shrugged. "Perhaps it was just a hunch."

Before Annie could answer, a maid she hadn't seen before wheeled a dinner cart into the room. She stopped by Hans first and put a plate before him, then placed a filet of beef on it, along with some *potatoes au gratin,* and a mix of green beans and almonds. She moved on to each of the little princesses before coming to Annie. A wine steward followed close behind, pouring a glass of red wine for both Hans and Annie. The children had milk.

"I had the most wonderful idea for where to take the children tomorrow," Annie said, slicing the deliciously aromatic filet before her. "What if we were to go to breakfast at that darling little patisserie in town, then take a brisk walk back to the palace? The weather has been—"

"Miss Barimer," Hans interrupted. "There are two problems with that. The first is that the children have their schooling from eight o'clock until two in the afternoon, so you couldn't possibly have them back on time."

"Oh." Annie had forgotten about the hours each day that the girls had their regular schooling. "Then we can go after school."

"Oh, could we, Father?" Marta said immediately, in German. Her eyes were pleading. "Please?"

"English," Hans told her. "And the answer is no. The royal princesses do not gallivant in the streets of Lassberg." He leveled his gaze on Besa, then Marta. "As you two are well aware, and you," he looked at Annie, "should be."

She was shocked. "Are you saying I can't take the children outdoors?"

He took a sip of wine, then gestured magnanimously with his glass. "Certainly you can. But you may not leave the palace grounds."

"Never?"

"Not unless there is an occasion that specifically calls for it."

"Do they *ever* go out in public to do ordinary, non-occasion things?"

"No," Marta said miserably.

Besa's eyes went wide.

Annie saw a reprimand coming from Hans and tried to divert it. "I mean, not even with you?"

He looked at her and sighed with impatience. "As I said, they go out when the occasion calls for it. Usually, it does not. It's simply not safe to have them walking around in public all the time."

Annie frowned. "Forgive my impertinence, but I've noticed there are guards around all the time. They're subtle but not invisible. Surely even the most paranoid person could feel safe with them around."

His eyes narrowed. "Miss Barimer, English is not my native language, so correct me if I'm wrong, but 'paranoid' is not precisely a term of admiration, is it?" He left no doubt that he knew exactly what paranoid meant.

She felt her face grow hot. That had been the wrong thing to say. Would she ever learn to use the kind of discretion that was necessary in a royal household? "I didn't mean to imply that you're paranoid, sir, honestly. I only meant that surely it would be safe to take them out once in a while. Wouldn't it?"

"Why go looking for trouble?" Hans asked, but it wasn't really a question. It was a dismissal of the subject. He looked down at his plate and went to work on his food.

Annie knew enough not to argue further.

She took a bite of some sort of cream sauce, and

her taste buds exploded. Her calculations of the pros of living in a royal household had not included this. She would probably gain fifteen pounds before her term was up, but she didn't care. She would enjoy putting on each and every one of them.

After a few minutes, she looked at Marta and asked, "What are you studying right now?"

She dabbed a napkin against her mouth. "I'm studying Napoleon Bonaparte and the French Revolution."

"Really? Are you enjoying it?"

Marta shrugged. "I must learn it."

"I'm studying monkeys," Besa chirped.

"Monkeys?" Annie repeated, frowning.

Hans thought for a moment. "Perhaps she's referring to Darwin's Theory of Evolution."

"My goodness."

"No, Father, Frau Henson is teaching Besa about currency. I think Besa has gotten the wrong word, that's all."

"It's not the wrong word," Besa argued. "Monkey."

"A monkey is an animal," Marta shot back. "Animals have nothing to do with currency."

"In English, the word is *monkey*." Besa looked like she was on the edge of tears. "Ask Miss Barimer."

"Ah, money," Annie said. "Yes, indeed, you were very close."

"That wasn't close," Marta said, miffed that she didn't get proper credit for knowing better.

"It's very close, just one letter off. But I'm impressed with you, Marta, your English is really quite good.''

''You're not the first English lady who's lived here,'' Marta said.

Annie felt an inexplicable pang. ''Well, whoever taught you did a very good job.''

''Our mother taught us. *She* spoke English as perfectly as the Queen of England.''

Hans put his knife and fork down. ''Miss Barimer, let us save conversation for another time, when we're not at the table, shall we?''

''Yes, of course.'' She paused, then said, ''Let me just get this straight. You don't talk at the table during dinner?''

''Not under normal circumstances, no.''

''Under normal circumstances you eat alone, so it would be weird for you to talk,'' Annie said, trying to clarify. ''I meant when you're with other people.''

He shot her a look that stopped her cold. ''We're here to eat, Miss Barimer. I suggest you do just that.''

It wasn't a subtle hint but she took it. She was beginning to understand how things worked around here. As she patted butter onto a hard roll, Annie thought that she'd already made so many mistakes in her first day here that she would probably be fired by morning. Why couldn't she just keep her mouth shut instead of always speaking her mind? It wasn't dishonest to have an unexpressed thought. She was going to have to remember that when dealing with Hans in the future.

* * *

It was nearly midnight and Hans was still in his office, idly doing paperwork that he should have done that afternoon. It was difficult to concentrate, ever since the shock of learning that Annie was Anastasia Barimer.

He had a terrible feeling that this situation wasn't going to work. Not that he was ready to fire her. How could he, when she'd just arrived from five-thousand miles away? She'd quit her job, left her home. If he let her go after just one day she would practically be out in the streets. From what he knew already, her pride would probably prevent her taking severance pay.

No, he'd have to see this through a bit longer.

He set his papers aside and stood up. It had been a long day, and tomorrow promised to be another one. And the day after that…probably. But he wasn't going to think that far ahead right now. Now he had other things to do.

Coffee would help. He stretched and left the room, walking through the silent halls toward the kitchen. A cuckoo clock in the south parlor ticked loudly. It had always annoyed him. One of these days he was going to have to get rid of it.

He stopped. Is that what I do? he asked himself. Get rid of treasures because they annoy me? Of course not. At least not in the callous way that implied.

Turning away from that thought, he continued on toward the kitchen, but now the clock's ticks measured his steps like some ominous movie theme music. He would be perfectly justified in getting rid of clocks and employees that didn't work the way he wanted them to. He had important matters of state to attend to, he didn't need distractions. Especially the kind of distractions that wouldn't amount to anything anyway. For instance, his problems with Annie would have no significance beyond an elevated blood pressure and perhaps the occasional bout of heartburn. Not bad for the state, but not good for him.

Leo had said the very same thing today when they'd been discussing a tricky export tax Hans had been working on for the past several months. Hans's mind kept wandering in Annie's direction and Leo had noticed it. Without even knowing the specifics, only seeing how it affected Hans, Leo had suggested—in quite strong terms—that they find a new teacher.

He'd told Leo that he wasn't willing to make such a radical move so soon, but he could see Leo's point. Annie was shaping up to be a lot more work than he'd anticipated.

A lot of the problem was her American upbringing, he reasoned. She'd said herself she was used to a different life-style. She probably grew up eating pot roast dinners around some provincial family dinner table and couldn't conceive of anything else.

True, he'd expressed an interest in the way Americans did things, but what he'd had in mind was the pioneering tradition, the conviction that all Americans seemed to have that they could change things, improve things, affect things. That kind of empowerment was what he wanted for his daughters. He'd have to make himself clear to Annie on that point.

She didn't understand what he wanted of her. That was at least partially his fault. He hadn't communicated his needs fully enough.

Feeling a little irritated with himself, he strode through the formal dining room and gave the swinging door to the kitchen a hard shove. It only opened halfway before it hit something solid.

There was a muffled exclamation on the other side, unmistakably feminine.

Hans opened the door outward and saw Annie standing there, looking at him in shock.

"I'm terribly sorry," he said immediately. He put a hand on her elbow to usher her over to a seat.

"It's okay, really," Annie said, stopping before he could get her to sit. A pink flush rose delicately in her cheeks. "You opened the door as I was walking past and it knocked into my foot." She pointed to a fluffy, orange slipper.

"Your foot?"

"Well, and my hip." She gave a quick laugh. "Fortunately, both are pretty well padded."

His eyes dropped to her hips. She was wearing a nightgown and robe, but the robe hung open and he could see the vaguest outline of her form beneath the thin fabric of her gown. She was definitely neither over- nor under-padded. In fact, she was just about perfect, at least as far as her physical proportions went. Which was just an objective observation, he told himself, not a personal one. He only noticed her…proportions because she brought it up.

Hans raised his gaze to her eyes and let out a

breath he hadn't realized he was holding. "Are you quite sure you're all right?"

She carefully secured her robe, then swallowed hard enough for him to notice. "Yes, fine."

What if he'd really injured her? He shuddered at the thought, relieved that she was okay.

He cleared his throat. "I hope you'll accept my apologies, then."

"Of course. I know you weren't trying to bump me off or anything."

"Bump you off?" Had he heard that expression before?

She smiled. "You know, get rid of me."

"Ah." In his head, he could already hear Besa and Marta parroting the expression. "Right. Of course not."

They stood facing each other in the darkened kitchen. The only light came from over the stove, and through the wall of windows that faced a landscape iridescent with snow. It would have been a romantic moment, under other circumstances. Even Hans could see that.

Desperate to change the subject, Hans gestured toward the table and chairs. "If you'd like to have a seat, I'll make you some coffee." He started to turn to the freezer.

She put out an arm to stop him, inadvertently loosening her robe as she did so, though she didn't notice. "Oh, please don't bother—"

He glanced at her then looked away tactfully. Not that she was indecently exposed. It was worse. There was just enough of her creamy skin showing, enough of her curves suggested, to drive a man's imagination mad.

"Oh!" He heard her tie it up again and looked to see that she was somewhat red-faced. "I'm sorry."

"About the coffee...?"

She shook her head. "Really, I don't want to trouble you."

"It's no trouble. I was going to make some anyway. Or try to." After the glimpse he'd just had of her, the chill of the freezer was just exactly what he needed to set his mind and body back on track. He went to the freezer, opened the heavy door and breathed in the frosty air. "I could make decaffeinated, if you prefer it." What was he doing? He specifically came to the kitchen to get some caffeine. Yet here he was, once again bending to make things better for Annie rather than himself. "I can make two pots," he finished, now disgusted with himself for the hoops he seemed to be jumping through.

"Well..."

"That is, unless you're anxious to get back to your room?" He paused and looked back at her. The shadows fell around her like dark cloaks, but she was a warm beacon in the midst of them. He was surprised at how her presence struck him.

He didn't want her to leave.

She hesitated, her gaze lingering on his, then looked at her watch. "You know, I—I'd like to stay, but I really should get to sleep. The girls have to be dressed and fed by eight in the morning." She smiled. "Don't want to mess up the first day of the job."

That was good. He was relieved that she was so eager to do the job, and do it well. He gave a bow of his head, conceding more than she could possibly understand. "I'm glad to see you're so conscientious."

She looked at the bag in his hand and frowned. "Before I go, would you like me to help?"

"Help?"

She nodded and gave a smile. It was a very nice smile. She probably needed it often after exasperating other people. "With the coffee," she said.

"Oh. No." He shook his head. "I don't need help, thank you."

She looked again at the bag he held and gestured. "But...those are frozen vegetables you're holding there."

He looked at the bag. It was a bag of frozen vegetables. The cook had gone overboard freezing and canning the summer harvest in September. The freezer was full of them and he'd grabbed the wrong thing. He gave a half a laugh. "Midnight snack."

She nodded uncertainly. "Oh."

"Sure you won't join me?"

"I'm sure." She pulled her robe closer around her. "Maybe another time."

He nodded, though it didn't seem like a good idea. He didn't want any of the lines between employer and employee blurred, and he had the feeling if anyone could blur the lines, Annie could. That thought made him smile ruefully. "Another time."

Chapter Five

"Is today a special occasion?" Annie asked, as Margaret poured her a steaming mug of coffee, then dropped a cube of dark chocolate in it. She and the girls were back in the formal dining room, minus Hans, and Margaret had just served tall, steaming hot waffles, with an assortment of fruit toppings, whipped cream, and syrup to top them.

"I don't think so. Why?"

Annie gestured at the spread. "All this food. Mocha."

Margaret laughed. "What, you didn't eat like this at home? This is every day fare for this lot. And for you, too, now."

"I'll weigh a ton by the end of the year," Annie predicted, pouring cream into her mocha and stirring it to a pale beige. The aroma that wafted from it was so rich she could taste it. "And I'll be as happy as a clam."

"Happy as a *clam?*" Besa repeated, after listening to the exchange. She looked puzzled.

"It's an expression," Annie explained with a smile. "Like 'snug as a bug in a rug,' have you heard that one?"

Both children looked horrified.

"I don't like bugs at all," Besa said.

"And I don't like the idea of having them in my rug," Marta said, scratching her head. "It makes me itch just thinking about it."

Annie nodded. It was going to be hard getting used to being around people who took everything she said literally. "It's not a very nice image, I suppose. But it's just an expression. A nice one, actually, meaning that one is completely and utterly content."

"Happy as a clam," Marta said, trying the phrase out. She glanced sidelong at Besa. "I like it."

"I like it, too," Besa shot back in German. "I just didn't understand it—"

"Girls," Annie said firmly. They stopped and looked at her. "This is one thing we have to get straight right up front. There will be no mocking one another for not understanding something, is that clear? I want you both to feel free to ask questions any time. That's the only way to learn."

"Very well."

"Yes, Miss Barimer."

Pleased that they had agreed to her terms without arguing, Annie switched the subject. "Today we're going to begin reading the story of Frances Willman, the little peasant girl who helped a wounded soldier back in the First World War, and stopped the fighting in Lassberg for a day. Are you familiar with it?''

"Father says that story is embellished. He says that girl took a foolish chance in going outdoors at a dangerous time and that many men might have been killed because of it.''

Annie bit her tongue. Until she could order the English and American books she'd been unable to pack, she'd planned to have the girls read the copy of *A Day of Peace* that she'd bought at the airport. "Perhaps, but she saved a life without regard for her own. That makes her a hero.'' In fact, it makes her bold. The very thing Hans said he admired in American children.

"You said she was a peasant,'' Besa said.

"You can be both,'' Marta told her.

"Oh.'' Besa looked at Annie with a furrowed brow. "What's a peasant?''

"That's an old-fashioned word for…'' How could she explain this? "For an ordinary person. Her family lived and worked in town and had no titles or royal position.'' The children continued to look confused. "In other words, she wasn't a princess like you and Marta.''

"I often wish I weren't a princess,'' Marta stated flatly, with a shake of her head that seemed far too old and resigned for her ten years.

"Why, Marta?'' Annie was touched by the girl's statement.

"We are not allowed to play with other children, or do any of the things we see children do on television." She sighed dramatically. "It's for our own safety."

"What would you like to do, if you could?" Annie prodded gently.

Marta considered this very carefully, as if she had only one more wish to ask of a genie. "I think I would like to go to a school with other children my age."

"I'd want to eat ice cream in the park!" Besa chirped before Annie could answer.

Annie smiled. "I don't know if I can do anything about your schooling, but we might be able to swing a day in the park sometime." Or do something to get you out of the confines of this palace so you can run around like average kids, she added to herself. Suddenly she thought of the memorial statue of the little peasant girl in Lassberg. It would be a perfect field trip.

"Really?" Besa asked, then shot a smug look at her sister. "I suggested the park," she said to her in German.

"English," Annie reminded her. "Remember we're supposed to be learning English." She cut a section of waffle on her plate, then gestured to the girls with her fork. "Eat up, now, you have to go to class in a few minutes."

They did, and Annie spent the rest of breakfast thinking about taking the girls into town and how she could talk Hans into allowing it.

"I'd like to see His Highness for a few minutes," Annie said to Greta outside Hans's office twenty minutes later.

Greta frowned. "Is everything all right?"

"Yes, fine. It's about taking the children on an outing."

"I see." Greta scanned the appointment book in front of her. "He might perhaps be able to see you at three o'clock this afternoon." She poised her pen over the page, waiting for Annie's answer so she could write it down.

Annie was taken aback. She hadn't expected to have to make an appointment to talk with Hans about his children. Then again, she hadn't expected to be working in the royal household at all, so all of this was new to her and she had to expect to be surprised by most things.

"Is there any way I could speak with him for just a couple of minutes now?" she asked. "I'm really terribly sorry, but it's important and it will only take a moment."

Greta gave a patient smile. "I do apologize, but His Highness is working and asked not to be disturbed."

"Miss Barimer, I presume," a sharp voice said behind Annie. Startled, she whirled to see a stocky, silver-haired man striding into the room. "Is there a problem?" he asked, in short, clipped English.

"Miss Barimer, this is Leo Kolbort, the prince's chief advisor," Greta explained gently, in a way that made it obvious to Annie that Leo was no picnic to deal with.

She steeled herself. "There's no problem, Mr. Kolbort. I just need to speak with Prince Johann for a moment."

"I believe I heard Greta say he was busy."

Leo's gruffness was disconcerting. She felt like a child being reprimanded by the school principal.

"I believe I heard that, too, thank you very much, but this is important." She turned back to Greta, but was brought up short by Leo's voice behind her.

"His Highness doesn't have the time to supervise every move you make, Miss Barimer. You were hired so that he might be able to run the country without stopping every hour to deal with his children. It is my job to help His Highness's work run smoothly. Therefore, I suggest that, if you are absolutely unable to use your own judgment in the future, you refer your questions to me, rather than to him. Now," he struck an expectant pose, "what is it you wish to know?"

The idea of facing this man every time she wanted to talk about the children was enough to make her shudder. "With all due respect, His Highness has said nothing to me about consulting you under any circumstances."

The little man's face grew red. "Miss Barimer, I am Prince Johann's top advisor, and as such I handle as many little annoyances for him as I can in order that he may work undisturbed—"

"What is going on out here?" Hans's voice sliced through the tension as sharply as a sword.

Annie whirled around and saw him standing, dark and commanding, in the open doorway of his office. His green eyes flicked from her to Greta to Leo, then back to Annie. Instead of feeling intimidated, though,

Annie felt strangely relieved. "Your Highness, I needed a moment with you and Colonel Klink here said I couldn't—"

"Kolbort," Leo snapped.

She wasn't sure but she thought she saw a tiny glint of amusement in Hans's eyes.

"He advised me to use my own judgment and I have decided to do just that." She smiled sweetly at Leo. "It was very good advice."

Hans frowned. "Then there is no problem?"

"No, no problem."

He glanced at Leo. "And I may get back to work?"

"Absolutely, sir, I apologize most humbly for the interruption."

Annie watched Leo's backpedaling in amazement.

Greta cleared her throat discreetly. "Your Highness, you have a telephone conference in five minutes. Shall I begin making the calls?"

When he smiled at Greta it was genuine, and Annie felt a short stab in her chest. If only he would smile at her that way.

"Yes, Greta." He looked from Leo to Annie, though his gaze lingered on Annie. "You will excuse me?"

A lump formed in her throat. "Of course," she said. "I'm sorry to have bothered you."

He gave a curt nod, but this time there was no doubt that the corner of his mouth lifted slightly.

She refused to run away like a dog with its tail between its legs. Instead, she took a steadying breath and looked at Greta. "There's just one more thing. I'll be needing a computer with Internet access."

"Of course," Greta said, without missing a beat. She went on to ask which server and programs Annie preferred, taking notes as she did. Both of them ignored Leo, who stood watching and listening like a prison guard.

When they were finished, Greta said, "This should not take long. I'll have it sent to your room, if that's all right with you."

"Great, thanks."

Feeling slightly more confident though still daunted by Leo's level gaze, Annie turned and left. She hoped that if she was going to drop dead of a heart attack, as the banging in her chest suggested, she would at least do it when she was out of his sight.

"Are you certain we're allowed to do this?" Besa asked worriedly as they walked down the hill into the town.

Marta thumped her lightly on the back of her heavy coat. "Don't cause trouble. This is the first time we've gotten to go outside without those infernal guards."

Annie smiled at Marta's use of her father's word, *infernal*. Moreover, she had used it correctly—even Annie was tired of the hovering presences of the guards in the palace, although she did feel a little trepidation about having left without them. They hadn't dodged the guards, precisely, they had just left through the door in the kitchen, rather than the front door that lead to the highly visible courtyard. It was faster to leave through the kitchen, that was all.

"Father said the maid is infernal, not the guards," Besa argued.

"No one is infernal," Annie said, bringing the argument to a halt. "That's not a kind thing to say about anyone. Your father was simply annoyed that something had been broken."

They walked on down a path through the snowy mountainside, breathing deeply the fresh, cool air. Along the way they told stories and giggled. As the lovely little town came into view, Annie thought she'd never felt so alive.

Although from the time they left the palace to the moment they stepped into the town square was only about fifteen minutes, the girls said they'd never done the walk before. Every time they left it was in an armored car.

"Can we do this every day?" Marta asked, swinging herself around a lamppost.

"Not every day," Annie said. "But we'll do lots of fun things together, I promise."

"Look!" Besa cried, pointing at the statue of a little girl. "That must be Frances Willman!"

"It is," Annie agreed. "Let's go take a closer look." She took a hand of each girl in her own and crossed the street to the statue. It was about four feet tall, cast in bronze, and made with exquisite detail, right down to her eyelashes, and the buttons on her peasant dress. A plaque at the base of the statue noted her as "The Little Girl of Peace."

They sat down on a bench near the statue and An-

nie took the book out of her bag and began reading
the story of Frances Willman to the girls. They listened with rapt attention until she closed the book
about twenty minutes later. Unfortunately, Annie
hadn't noticed that, while she was reading, people
had gathered around them and were staring and whis-
pering. It was only when she'd put the book back in
her bag that she noticed the two burly police officers
coming toward her.

"What are you doing with the Royal Princesses?"
one asked in gruff German. "Who are you?"

The other went to the girls and put a protective
hand on each one's shoulder.

"Miss Barimer?" Besa asked in a frightened
voice.

"It's all right, darling," Annie reassured her. Then
to the police, she said in German, "I'm Anastasia
Barimer, the children's English tutor. We've just
come to town on a sort of," she tried to think of the
German for 'field trip,' "'adventure.' To learn the
history of Lassberg."

The big man's face grew darker, if possible.
"We've had no word from the palace about this."

Suddenly the stupidity of slipping out the back
door without anyone's knowledge hit Annie full-
force. Some judgment she'd used. "I didn't think to
notify you," she explained. "I'm new to this job,
you see, and, well, I didn't even know it was for the
royal family until I got here, so there's an awful lot
to learn, I'm afraid." She was babbling. "But next
time I'll be sure to notify you before we leave the
grounds."

"The palace secretary always notifies us when the royal family is on an approved excursion."

Annie gave the most confident smile she could, realizing that the officers were only doing their jobs and that this whole mess could be cleared up as soon as they understood that she was who she said she was. "Ah, yes, the palace secretary. I should have notified her before we left but, well, I just didn't think of it." She turned to the policeman who was with Marta and Besa. "I'm sure if you call her, she'll tell you I'm on the up and up. That is, she'll tell you that I'm allowed to have the girls." Greta would back her up, she was sure of it.

He looked at the other officer and said something about calling, then took out a two-way radio. He told the dispatcher to call the palace secretary for confirmation, and the dispatcher told him to stand by.

"I'm really sorry to put you through all of this," Annie said, trying to ignore the crowd that had gathered around them. She swallowed. "Next time I'll be more careful."

The officers didn't answer.

"I'm tired of guards," Besa said, trying to step away from the uniformed policeman. "I thought we snuck away from them!"

Annie felt her face grow hot. "Besa, we didn't *sneak* away. Don't give the officers the wrong idea."

"Are we in trouble?" Marta asked Annie, her face pale.

"No, of course not. Greta, I mean Frau Entemain will clear all of this up for us and then we'll go home."

There was a static burst from the radio as the dispatcher called for attention. The officer spoke for a moment, then turned off the radio and put it in his pocket.

"So can we go now?" Annie asked.

He shook his head. "I'm afraid not."

"You know, I don't want to get contentious with you, since I know you're trying to do your job, but I think this is against the law. I could probably sue the whole police department for this—" she looked around at the crowd, "this public humiliation. And being held against my will."

"You cannot sue us, Miss. This is not like America."

"Then," she scrambled desperately, "Prince Johann will have your heads. He'll be furious when he finds out what you're doing. And in front of the children."

He ignored her and took something out of an inner pocket. To her horror, she realized it was handcuffs. There was a flash as someone took a picture.

"Take the children to the station," he said to his partner. "Someone is coming to pick them up."

"Wait a minute!" Annie cried, realizing her threats were getting her nowhere. "I thought you were calling the palace secretary. Greta Entemain."

"We spoke with a palace official," he said vaguely, clamping the cold metal around her wrists. "Herr Kolbort was very concerned about the matter indeed."

Annie felt as though she'd been punched in the stomach. "Herr Kolbort?"

He nodded.

"He told us," the first officer said slowly and deliberately, "that the princesses were absolutely not allowed to be off the palace grounds."

She couldn't believe her ears. Things were spiraling rapidly out of control, and there was nothing she could do to stop it. "No, no, you must have misunderstood him."

The officer leveled an icy gaze on her. "There was no mistake."

With a short shake of his head, the officer began reciting what she assumed were the Kublenstein equivalent of her Miranda rights.

"What's going on?" she interrupted.

He stopped and frowned dramatically. He was clearly relishing the idea of being a hero to Hans and his country by saving the princesses. "You, miss, are under arrest for kidnapping the royal children."

Chapter Six

The prison cell was just like a dungeon of old, with thick stone block walls, and a tiny, high window that let in a slight milky haze of light. There was a hard cot for a bed and that was it. It possessed absolutely none of the charms of popular lore. No guard stood sentry at the end of the hall as in a medieval fable, no cheerful drunk was there to take the key from Barney Fife and open the door as in *The Andy Griffith Show*. It was just Annie, alone in a torturous cubicle underground.

But she wasn't worried about herself, though perhaps she should have been—if Leo would allow her to be arrested as a kidnapper, who knew what else he might do—she was more worried about Besa and Marta. She paced back and forth, trailing her hands along the cold prison bars, thinking about how she might help the children. They were in safe hands, she was sure, but they were probably frightened and confused, and that would linger long after this momentary detention. The pleasant trip into town that they had been so excited about had turned into a nightmare. Annie hoped it wouldn't frighten them to the point that they withdrew further into their sheltered lives, but it was a possibility and for that she was really angry at Leo. And herself. Why hadn't she thought? They were royalty, after all. Yes, they were children, but their position set them apart. She couldn't treat them like ordinary kids.

She sat down on the lumpy cot and leaned against the craggly stone wall. It cut into her shoulder blade and she shifted in an effort to get more comfortable but she couldn't. Finally she just lay down, as the lumpy mattress was preferable to the treacherous wall and wondered if they'd call the American Embassy or if she should.

The day's experience must have been more exhausting than she'd realized because the next time she opened her eyes the light from the window was gone and there was a loud rattling at the end of the hall where a door was being unlocked.

Annie sat up quickly, trying to orient herself.

The door opened and Hans came walking through, trailed by several guards. She knew he'd be angry with her, nevertheless her heart soared as if he were a knight riding up on a white steed. Never mind that there was a hard glint in his eye, detectable from ten yards away. Anger she could take. Fifty years in this prison she could not. He was going to spring her!

He walked up to the cell door and studied Annie

for a moment before speaking. "When you said my daughters needed to learn about the real world," he said deliberately, "did you have prison specifically in mind or is this merely an added bonus to your curriculum?"

Whatever inner strength had been holding her together collapsed like a house of cards. "I'm so sorry about this," she said, ashamed to find herself close to tears. "It was all one big horrible misunderstanding. I'm so, so sorry."

His face remained impassive. "I thought I was quite clear on the point of keeping the children at home."

She sniffed. "Well, this was meant to be an educational field trip."

"For which you did not have consent."

She nodded slowly. "I went to your office this morning for that very reason."

He raised an eyebrow and shifted his weight. "But you knew I wouldn't agree, so you left without discussing it with me at all."

"No," she said firmly, taking hold of the chilly bars. "Absolutely not. Leo wouldn't let me speak with you. He said I was hired to take charge of the children and that I should use my own discretion, as I was hired to do, rather than trouble you with minor details."

"I would hardly call this," he gestured at the prison bars, "a minor detail."

She sighed. "No, it isn't, as it turned out. Of course I didn't intend to get arrested and have the children spend the afternoon in a police station. But it should have been a simple excursion. An educational excursion.''

He gave a slight shake of the head. ''It was a flagrant disregard of the rules I set out for you.''

''That,'' Annie said, stepping back from the bars, ''is not true. I was told by Leo that I was to decide what was best myself. And while we're on the subject of Leo,'' better he was on the defensive than the offensive, ''why did he tell the police he didn't know who I was when they called?''

Hans gave an unconcerned shrug. ''I have spoken to Leo about his lapse in judgment. He assured me he just didn't connect your name with the children's.''

''I find that very hard to believe, particularly after our exchange just a few hours ago.''

There was a long silence during which Annie hoped Hans was building toward a concession of some sort. Instead, he drew himself up and gestured back toward the door he'd come in through. ''They're just finishing some paperwork and someone will be along with the key.''

''Good.''

Another silence hung between them.

''I expect you'll follow the rules henceforth,'' he said in a hard tone.

She was loathe to commit to something she didn't believe in her heart was in the best interest of the girls. ''I promise you I won't do anything to endanger the children,'' she worded cagily. ''It was foolish of me to take them out without anyone knowing where we were going. I just wasn't thinking. Believe me, I've learned my lesson.''

''I hope so.''

A chubby guard came through the door then, jingling keys on a large round chain. When he saw Hans, he looked startled and gave a slight bow, then another as he passed, and yet another after he'd passed. Despite her situation—or perhaps because of it—Annie had to suppress a giggle.

The guard opened the door and she nearly ran through it. She felt as though she'd been locked up forever. Impulsively she reached out and hugged Hans. ''Thank you. You're really my hero.''

She felt him straighten in her embrace, then relax fractionally. When he started to hug her back, a warm shiver went through her. ''That's going a bit far.''

She drew back. ''No, really, if you hadn't come here personally, who knows how long it would have taken for them to spring me? Heck, if you'd sent Leo I would have been sitting in there for days.''

''It's good I didn't send Leo, then,'' he responded, looking thoughtful again. ''I'll bear that in mind in the future.''

Annie was turning out to be a complete catastrophe. Worse, even, than Hans could have imagined.

She'd disobeyed his word. She'd endangered his children. She'd deceived the entire household in sneaking the royal princesses outside.

She'd *hugged* him.

He pounded his hands down on his desk and stood

up. It was late. Everyone had left the office hours ago, and most of the lights were dimmed. He didn't care. The alternative to work was to go have dinner with Annie and the girls, and he just didn't want to face her right now. She was too exasperating. And appealing.

He sighed and looked around the room for something to distract his attention. There was nothing, except for the rather large police report that had been delivered a few hours earlier. He'd have to look at it eventually, he realized, and sign-off on the papers. But not now.

He muttered an oath and walked over to the window, to at least get a change of scenery. He looked out at the curved drifts of snow glowing softly in the light of the outdoor lamps. The clouds had gathered again in the early evening and now tiny flakes were drifting to the ground. He leaned against the sill and watched them.

As a child, he'd always felt a thrill when the snow came, even though he wasn't allowed to go outdoors and play the way other children did. He wasn't sure whether it was a matter of safety, or simply a matter of being the only child in a stuffy household of adults and protocol. Whatever it was, it had made for a lonely childhood. Still, the snow had always made the world look like a wonderland. He could imagine running out into it, pulling a sled up a hill, stopping for steaming hot chocolate.... Later, of course, he'd learned to ski and become proficient in all the winter sports he'd dreamed of as a child, but it never quite measured up to the fun he'd imagined it would have been as a young boy.

He unlatched the window and pushed it open a sliver. The room had grown stuffy. The cool metallic scent touched his nostrils and sent a rush of energy through him. His muscles yearned to run and stretch. But there was no time for that nonsense now.

Just as he turned to go back to his desk, a shout below on the grounds caught his attention.

"You're it!" It was Marta's voice, undoubtedly. Her shriek had an urgent note to it.

He rushed back to the window and looked out just in time to see a small ball of snow plummet into Besa's back and explode into a little white cloud. "Nooooo!" she squealed, then crumpled into a shuddering ball on the ground.

He was running down the hall before he'd even stopped to think about his actions. He had to get to the children. Where was Annie? Why wasn't she there to protect them? This was really the end. He'd been inclined toward lenience, even after this afternoon's debacle in the town square, but *this* was the final straw. The children were being attacked under his very nose, and Annie was allowing it!

He slammed through the kitchen door, hearing a crash behind him but he didn't stop to see what it was. He didn't care if every piece of china flew off the shelves, he had to get to his daughters.

When he got to the back door, breathless and tense, he stopped short. Annie was there. In fact, a puff of snow was ricocheting off her shoulder as she came into view, and her hair was covered with it.

Her dark coat was dotted with splotches of it. And she was laughing.

"I got you!" Marta cried.

Hans's heart pounded as adrenaline continued to course through his veins, but when he looked at his children something didn't compute. It wasn't fear in their faces, as he'd expected. They weren't crying and trembling with fear. It was something far more rare for them.

It was joy he was seeing and hearing. They were laughing, and Annie was laughing right along with them as they pounded snow into balls and tossed them at each other, barking with triumph every time they hit their mark.

Next they trotted over to some clean snow and fell backwards into it, moving their arms and legs like flopping fish. Annie got up, and carefully helped each girl up, too. When they stepped back, the design they'd left surprised him. Angels. Three angels in the snow.

His heart clenched.

They continued to play for several minutes, unaware of his presence on the doorstep. Besa and Marta kept slipping in and out of English, but Annie guided them gently back every time they got it wrong.

"That's angels, Besa, not angles."

"Is it magic?" Besa asked, obviously still awestruck at the sight.

Annie laughed. It was a pretty laugh, echoing off the cold walls of the palace and making everything seem warmer including his own heart. "No, it's not magic, it's just…well, snow angels. You two have really never done that before?''

''No. How did you learn?''

Annie shrugged and gave another laugh. ''I don't know. Every kid in America knows how to make snow angels. It's just part of being a kid.''

Hans couldn't help stepping forward. ''We are not,'' he said, trying to hold back a smile which would—he told himself—have been one of relief only and not pleasure, ''in America.''

They all looked at him, startled.

Annie was the first to regain her composure. ''Then I've brought a little of America to you.'' She gestured at the snow angels with a mittened hand. ''Care to try one?''

He shook his head, resisting the temptation he felt in his heart. ''It goes against my nature.'' He raised an eyebrow. ''Or so I'm told.''

She smiled and met his eyes. ''It doesn't hurt to go against your nature every once in a while. At least not if it means lightening up and having some fun.''

Something between them connected and he nearly smiled back. But he couldn't give in that way. She was an employee, nothing more, and he had to treat her with detachment. That was what he'd always been taught with regards to palace employees, to keep an emotional distance. ''I disagree,'' he said, although he wasn't entirely sure he meant it.

Suddenly something freezing cold hit his cheek and slid down his neck inside his shirt.

He realized what it was immediately, and turned,

with disbelief, in the direction from which it had come.

"You're it," Besa said with a wide smile. Her eyes were so bright he could tell it from ten feet in the dark.

"I beg your pardon?" he asked deliberately, though he could tell his daughter wasn't going to be intimidated by him this evening. He had to remind himself that he had to exercise authority.

"We're playing snowball tag," she explained, with the infinite patience of a child.

Something in his heart melted. "Is that right?"

She nodded eagerly, clearly pleased at the idea that he might play with them. "I touched you with the snowball so now you're it."

He paused dramatically. "I'm the Crown Prince of Kublenstein," he said, barely smiling. "I am always *it*."

Annie laughed.

He turned to face her and her laughter grew even harder until she was doubled over with it. He had honestly never seen anything like it. It seemed to crack the gray walls around them and send them tumbling down, leaving warmth and color in their place.

Most of the time, people were so reserved around Hans that he could barely tell they were human. It was something he'd taken for granted since childhood. But Annie was different, and she made everything around her different. As a result, she would undoubtedly change life at the palace.

The odd thing was, Hans didn't entirely mind it. It was refreshing to be around someone who wasn't afraid to disagree with him, even though she did sometimes disagree rather strenuously. It was interesting how unpredictable life had become, even in small ways. Just this morning, he'd found himself a little more eager to get up and start his day, just to see what would happen.

Annie had been bright and irreverent on the train, and he'd liked her then, he really had. Perhaps it had something to do with the fact that he'd thought he'd never see her again, but he had gotten a real kick out of their conversation about Kublenstein and her perceptions of it. When she'd entered his office as the new English teacher, he'd been shocked, of course, but in retrospect he realized that it hadn't been an unpleasant shock. Even then she'd raised his curiosity. Hiring her had broken his routine, and he realized now that he had been very tired of it.

"Miss Barimer," he said, watching her face light up as she laughed. "Are you laughing at me?"

"I'm not laughing at you," she said, wiping tears from her cheeks. "I'm laughing with you."

"Ah." He wanted to reach out to her, to pull her to him. "Yet I'm not laughing."

"Oh, yes, you are," she said, irreverently. "No one says something like, 'I'm the Crown Prince of Kublenstein, I am always it,' seriously."

"Do you deny any of that?" he asked, straight-faced.

This sent her into further gales of laughter. "No! That's what makes it so funny."

What would it feel like, he wondered, to just give in to the urge to take her in his arms? What would it be like to kiss her? He was overwhelmed by the urge to try. But he couldn't. He wouldn't.

Instead he bent down slowly and picked up a handful of snow. "I'm it, eh?" he asked, packing the snow lightly into a ball. This was truly most unbecoming to his station. But at the moment, he didn't care.

Annie saw what he was doing and took a step back. "Besa tagged you, so, yes, you're it."

He kept his eyes steadily on her, although his daughters were already giggling and dashing off into the snow drifts. "And the object of this game is that I touch someone with this snow, yes?" He took several even steps toward her.

She took a short breath, without moving. "That's the object. You have someone in particular in mind?"

"As a matter of fact, I do." Quite a lot lately. God, she was lovely. Maybe it was the soft light, or the drifting snow, or the crisp chill in the air, but suddenly Annie looked delicious enough to eat.

And he was hungry.

"Let's do more snow angels," he heard Marta say from the pale distance.

"Oh, let's!" Besa agreed, and there were two muted thuds as they dropped in the snow.

He scanned the landscape until he saw their two inky forms in the snow and was confident they were safe. Then, without warning, his thoughts returned to Annie and how easily and wonderfully she could warm him up right now.

The woman was exasperating, impetuous and stubborn as a mule, but he had to admit, she was also extremely intelligent. She was unbearably opinionated, although, often correct. And she didn't have nearly the reverence for his position that he expected.

Still, there was something about her... Something he couldn't let go.

Three more steps and he was directly in front of her. She tilted her face up toward his, her lips parted temptingly. Parts of him flared to life with a heat unbecoming the cold atmosphere. Those parts couldn't be indulged however. Other parts of him had been too cold for too long.

Annie shivered.

"Cold?" he asked her.

"Not exactly."

"You want to give up?"

"Never." She smiled.

For a fleeting moment, he thought he could fall in love with her. If he was the type to fall in love, that was. But he wasn't.

"Then." He reached for her hand and pressed the snow into her mitten, "I believe you're it."

Chapter Seven

The snow was still damp in Hans's hair and clothes half an hour later when he returned to his office to look over the police report. Though the entire incident had taken no longer than four hours, the report consisted of at least fifty pages. He cringed at the manpower and time that had been wasted in putting the report together.

As he leafed through the pages, he realized it was a little worse than he'd feared. Annie had threatened to sue the police. What was she thinking? He read on, and felt his stomach clench when he got to the part where she'd threatened that Hans himself would "have their heads."

If the newspapers got ahold of that information, it would look very bad. Especially since he had championed her by going personally to the police station to have her released from prison. Leo had tried strenuously to stop him, but Hans had insisted on going. He'd felt responsible in a way. Knowing she'd be scared and confused by what had happened… well…he'd wanted to go himself and make it better. To make right any wrong he may have inadvertently created, he told himself.

Yet he was beginning to suspect, deep down, that there was something else happening.

Anyway, he should have known that, with Annie, things were never that simple. It was just like her to threaten the police. He'd have laughed if it weren't so serious. Granted, in her country, things were different. She was used to having the power to threaten lawsuits or action against injustice. She was used to being able to make her own decisions without all the complications that being a royal created.

That was where he'd made his mistake. Though he'd liked the idea of his daughters having an American influence, there was no way an American could understand the position of the royal family in society. Annie wouldn't know what was expected of either the children or herself until she was told. He hadn't taken into account the fact that an American woman would be so used to living independently that perhaps she couldn't adapt to life in and around a palace.

There was only one thing he could do.

He had to let her go.

He sat down at his desk and took a pad of paper and gold pen from the drawer. With a heavy sigh, he began to write.

Dear Ms. Barimer,
I realize this may be something of a surprise,
but in thinking over our business relationship, I
have decided that it would be in the best interest
of all to end your employment now. Clearly,
things are not working—

Hans stopped writing and crumpled the paper, then
threw it into the trash can on top of several others
just like it. This was getting him nowhere. He could
stop and wait for Greta to help him in the morning.
Her input, and her shorthand, would probably make
the process go more smoothly. But he couldn't wait,
he had to get this done now. Every time he hesitated
with Annie, he lost his determination.

He poised his pen over the paper once again, then,
again, he paused.

Perhaps it would be easier to speak with her in
person. He considered the idea, then dismissed it. It
would be worse to meet with her. Somehow she always turned things around when they spoke in person. Black looked white and down seemed like up
through the filter of Annie's perspective. And if he
wrote her a letter, he wouldn't have to look upon her
lovely face when he told her she would have to leave.

Besides, their contract called for written notice of
termination. His attorney had felt quite strongly
about it, as an irate ex-employee could claim all
kinds of things without written documentation. While
he didn't think Annie was the type to invent charges
against him, people could sometimes surprise you.
After all, he wouldn't have thought she was the type

to go against his word and...yes, he did. He knew from the moment he realized Annie was to be the teacher he'd employed that she was exactly the type of woman who would disregard authority in order to do what she thought was best.

He did believe her intentions had been good. It was her judgment that had been poor. This time everything had turned out all right. Next time it might not. That was why he had to dismiss her. It was nothing personal. It certainly had nothing to do with the way she confused things whenever she was around him. It definitely didn't have to do with the warm feeling he felt whenever she was around either.

He took out another sheet of paper and started over, but the next version read too much like a betrayal from a friend. He didn't want to upset her unnecessarily. He didn't even bother crumpling the paper this time, he just pushed it off his desk and let it float down into the trash.

When he started writing again, it was inspired. He knew exactly what to say, and how he wanted to say it.

Dear Ms. Barimer,
It is with great regret that I write this letter to terminate your employment—

A tiny knock at his office door sent the thoughts flying from his mind and he dropped the pen in disgust.

''Yes, what is it?'' he asked irritably.

The door opened a crack and Annie herself poked

her head in. "I'm sorry to interrupt you, but may I have a word?"

He was speechless for a second or two, then gestured her in. "You may," he said hesitantly, frowning and wondering what on earth had drawn her here at this particularly awkward moment.

She stepped in and closed the door quietly behind her. Though it was close to 11:00 p.m., she was dressed in fitted black pants and a black turtleneck sweater, as if she had just spent the day on the ski slopes. In fact, she looked like a model for one of the ski resorts. Except, of course, for the fact that her feet were bare. Somehow it fit her to stop just short of what he expected her to be.

"Look, I know it's late and that you were probably busy working on something, and I know we've already seen each other since…this afternoon…but," she stopped, shrugged and dropped her arms at her sides. "I just feel so bad about what happened. I had to apologize again before going to bed."

He considered his options, then realized, with some alarm, that he didn't have any options before him. "Miss Barimer, apologies are not—"

"Oh, but they are. They really are."

"I beg your pardon?"

She dipped her head, then looked back up at him. "I've done it again, I'm sorry. My father always told me I interrupted too much." She gave a small smile. "I thought you were going to say that apologies weren't necessary."

"Apologies aren't necessary," he repeated in disbelief. He'd been about to say that apologies were not going to make up for what had happened. Before he could go any further, she interrupted him again.

"That's really very generous of you. I don't know many men who would be so understanding, under the circumstances." She met his eyes and took a slow breath. "Perhaps I shouldn't say so, but I sensed you were different from the moment I first met you. Although I guess your faith in people shouldn't surprise me. I suppose that's one of the things that makes your people think so highly of you as a leader."

He didn't know what to say. He tried to tell himself it was a language problem, but he knew full well that if he could muster something in his own language she would have understood it. He tried again in English. "Perhaps I didn't express my expectations adequately when you began work here. For that, I sincerely apologize. However, I never could have imagined the circumstances that have arisen since you began."

"Don't blame yourself," Annie said, holding a hand up to silence him. "I know it's my fault that things haven't been going well. As a matter of fact, I even considered resigning."

He raised an eyebrow and shifted in his seat. This was interesting. Very interesting. "Did you?"

She nodded solemnly. "I considered it briefly, that's all. Don't worry, I'm going to honor my commitment to you and Besa and Marta."

Oh, no. "So you're saying…"

She nodded. "I'm staying. There's no way on

earth I'd let them down. Or you,'' she added tentatively.

"There's one thing I'd really like to know," Hans said, lacing his fingers in front of him.

"What's that?"

"Why do you repeatedly defy authority?"

Her defenses went up quickly, "Herr Kolbort told me not to bother you with—"

Hans held up a hand. "Let me restate my question. Why are you so determined that the children have what you regard as a 'normal' life, even though that means breaking the rules more often than not."

She considered for a moment before answering. "Because I don't believe the rules were made with any recognition of how important it is for the children to be nurtured, and to be shown the world and the way things work by someone who cares about them."

"So you think you know better."

She nodded. "Yes, I do."

"May I ask why?"

She hesitated.

"I'm very serious," Hans said, indicating a chair in front of his desk. "If you'd like to take a seat and explain this to me, I'll listen."

She put her hand on the back of the chair, appeared to think it over for a minute, then sat down. She sighed. "I told you already that I had a very close family when I was young, and that it meant a lot to me."

He nodded.

She cleared her throat gently. "Well, the reason I

know the value so well is that when I was twelve my father died suddenly." Her eyes softened and she looked down in her lap."

"I'm sorry," Hans found himself saying. Obviously it still affected her. Her pain was almost tangible, and he felt something stir in his own chest.

She looked back at him. She wasn't crying, but an inner torment was drawn on her face. "After that, everything changed. Just like that," she snapped her fingers, "my entire world collapsed, to say nothing of what it did to my mother. She had to go to work full-time. We had to move out of our home into a small apartment in a part of town that could be unsavory. I almost never got to see Mom, and when I did, she was exhausted." Her voice caught and she stopped.

Hans didn't know what to say. It was so far outside his own experience that he was left speechless, but with an overwhelming desire to make it all better for Annie. Something even he, in his ancient palace, couldn't do. "So you had to take care of yourself from that time?" he asked.

She shrugged. "My grandmother moved in, but she wasn't very mobile. I've often thought that made it harder for my mother, not easier."

It occurred to Hans that if he'd known her then, he could have solved so many of her problems with his resources. He was surprised to feel a pang of regret that he hadn't.

Annie continued. "When we moved, we lived in a neighborhood where there were lots of kids with working and absentee parents. I don't want to make a sweeping generalization, but it's true that the kids without so much attention weren't as happy, and they tended to get into trouble more. And so often they were neglected because their parents just didn't want to bother. There's nothing sadder.''

For a moment, all they heard was the clock ticking.

''Anyway,'' she placed her hands on her thighs and took a deep breath, ''I didn't mean to get so personal. My point is that I've been on both sides of the fence, and I've really seen how important personal attention is. Forget the big birthday gifts and special events. Kids need someone within shouting distance when they get stuck on a math problem.''

He hadn't realized he'd held his breath until he expelled it. ''I think I understand what you're saying now.'' Another moment passed. ''How is your mother today?''

''She died a few years ago,'' Annie said softly. ''It was soon after I started work at Pendleton. I think she waited to make sure I'd be all right.'' She smiled. ''It's too bad she can't see me now, huh?''

''I'm sure she'd be very proud.''

They sat and stared into each other's eyes for a moment.

''Anyway,'' Annie said, clapping her hands together. ''That's all I wanted to say. Actually, it's more than I meant to say. I'm sorry for what I did, and I promise you that your faith in me will be rewarded.''

''I'm sure it will.''

''Thanks.'' She smiled, and the way it lifted the

corners of her eyes made his chest tighten and his mouth go dry.

"So we are agreed that you will consult me with any questions about the children from now on?"

She nodded. "Absolutely."

It was easy to maintain detachment at this moment when the thought that he wasn't going to lose her made his heart beat faster; but he had to. "We cannot have another day like today."

She shook her head emphatically. "I promise I'll speak with you before I ever do anything even remotely objectionable again."

"Good." That was that.

She stopped at the door and looked back at him, far more alluringly than she'd intended, he was sure. "By the way, that was fun tonight. I'm glad you came out and joined us." A moment passed before she added, quickly, "It meant the world to Besa and Marta."

His throat felt tight. "I enjoyed it, too," he said. He cleared his throat and she returned her gaze to him. He raised his brows. "Was there anything else?"

"No, nothing else."

"Good night, then," he said, giving a small polite smile before returning his attention to the blank papers before him on the desk.

"Good night," he heard her say before the door clicked open and, a second later, shut.

So she was staying.

That was good.

But it was up to him to help her learn the ropes,

so to speak. He would try to educate her to be the kind of teacher he wanted his children to have. It couldn't be that difficult, after all she was a smart woman and she cared about Besa and Marta. Surely she would want to do what was best for them once she saw what that was. He was certain of it.

A small optimism lit like a match in the back of his mind. Whether or not he was the cause of the problems with Annie, he began to think he might hold the solution.

"I have an engagement at the opera tonight," Hans told Annie several weeks later. "I'd like you to attend with me."

"Tonight? But the girls have to get up so early—"

"Not the children, just you. For *educational purposes*," he emphasized, lifting one of her own phrases. "For you to see the kind of life the royal princesses will be leading, so that you may better prepare them as their teacher."

"Oh. I see." She flushed hotly and looked down at the floor so he wouldn't notice. Ever since the night in the snow, she hadn't been able to get Hans the man—as opposed to Prince Johann—out of her mind. An evening out together wasn't going to make the situation any better.

"Do you have something suitable to wear?"

"Yes, I—I think so." With Coco Chanel's words echoing in her mind, she had brought a simple black dress. It was the kind of thing that could be dressed up or down, Joy had assured her, so she assumed it could be made suitable for an evening at the opera, if there was really no way she could get out of it.

Not that she really wanted to get out of it.

"Good," Hans was saying dismissively. "Be ready to leave at seven-thirty this evening."

"But…"

He looked at her, as though surprised she was still in the room. "Yes?"

"Is this a dinner thing, or should I eat first?" It struck her immediately that there was probably a more eloquent way to have asked that—she was talking to a prince for Pete's sake—but she hoped the language difference kept it from sounding as casual to his ears as it had to hers.

The smile that bent the right side of his mouth told her that he'd caught her nuances completely. "It's an after-dinner thing," he said, his curved mouth more gorgeous than she'd realized before.

"Very well," she said, over-compensating. "I shall see you this evening."

With a light of amusement clear in his eyes, he bowed his head. "I shall look forward to it."

As he walked away, Annie wondered if he was making fun of her. Then she wondered if she minded. The truth was, his attention gave her a thrill.

And that was a problem. As fun as it was to have an office crush, when the office was the Royal Palace of Kublenstein and the crush was the Crown Prince, the result could only be trouble as she raced back to her room to take a digital photo of the outfit she intended to wear. A laptop computer had been delivered the previous afternoon, presumably while Annie was with the police. She plugged it in and started it up, glad to see the familiar Internet program pop up in the start menu. She slipped the disk in and uploaded the picture to Joy, with a frantic plea to help her make it an appropriate outfit for the opera.

Later that afternoon, when she checked her e-mail, Annie was pleased to see a response from Joy had already come in.

Subject: The Opera!
Date: 11/15/99 10:46:41 PM Eastern Daylight Time
From: JoyS@Pendleton.org
To: AnnieBar@ool.com

I cannot believe you're going to the opera with Prince Johann! Maybe I should get one of those royalty magazines and see if I can find your picture after this. Too bad he's not big enough to make CNN!

Okay, your outfit: it looks really good. As I remember, that dress fits you wonderfully, so don't cover it up! Leave it simple. Wear sheer black hose and some strappy black shoes, not those clunkers you had pictured with it. No jewelry, just your simple diamond stud earrings. Put your hair up. I know you don't think it looks good, but it does and you're going to the opera, for Pete's sake. Keep your make-up simple, but elegant. Use eyeliner, whether you want to or not. It will look striking and that, I assume, is what you want.

You'd better call me afterwards and tell me all about it.

—Joy

P.S. I can see it now, Princess Anastasia (ha ha).

Annie hit reply and sent a quick note thanking Joy and promising to supply details later, then she shut down the computer and went to her closet. She didn't have the strappy black shoes Joy had described, but she did have a pair that was a little more delicate than the pumps Joy had seen. She took them out and put them by the dress, along with a pair of sheer, black panty hose.

Excitement started to drum in her as she took off her clothes and headed for the shower. It was nearly six o'clock. In two hours she'd be out with Hans. It was practically a date, even if it was for business reasons. It would feel like a date.

As she lathered the shampoo into her hair, she couldn't help imagining running her fingers through Hans's thick dark hair. Which was a ridiculous thought but she enjoyed it anyway. She knew exactly what it would feel like, even though she'd never dated anyone who looked remotely like him. She could imagine a lot of things about touching Hans, actually. She could imagine a lot about Hans touching her, too.

Before she knew it, her imagination had run away with her and she had stayed in the shower so long she began to wrinkle like a prune. She shut off the water and dried off, putting on a terry cloth robe. When she opened the door to her bedroom, a puff of white steam entered the room with her. The clock on her bedside table said it was six-thirty. She still had plenty of time to get dressed. That was good. It would give her the opportunity to take her time and to stay calm.

She went to the window with her hairbrush and gazed out over the increasingly-familiar landscape. Acres and acres of nothing but nature beyond the deserted back drive. The view from her apartment in Virginia had been of a long-abandoned gas station and a modern drug store.

She thought of Hans and wondered what it had been like for him growing up here. Her impression was that it had been lonely. Something about him still struck her as lonely, although he did a good job of covering it up with bluster sometimes. She sighed. She liked Hans. Deep down, she thought she understood him.

Dangerous thinking, she realized.

Setting the brush down, she turned from the window and stood up, dropping her robe behind her as she walked to the bed. She picked up the underwear she'd laid out with her clothes and put them on.

As she pulled her stockings on, her skin rose in prickly gooseflesh although the room was quite warm. She wondered what it would be like to have him touching her…

She pushed the thought away.

She was an intelligent woman, and far too mature to be indulging in these silly fantasies about her boss.

Shaking off the feeling, she continued to dress, but now she felt just a little disconcerted.

Something told her it might be a very long night ahead.

"I want to use the Rolls tonight," Hans said to Christian early that evening.

"The Rolls?" the driver repeated. "I'm sorry, sir, I had the other car prepared. I wasn't aware this was a special occasion."

Hans thought of Annie. "The Rolls. Clean it up and make sure there's enough fuel to take the scenic route to Geneva."

Christian gave him a puzzled look, but nodded. "Yes, sir."

Hans began to walk away, then stopped and turned back. "And Christian, if you could have a bottle of champagne on ice in the back, I'd appreciate it."

"Yes, sir."

It was perfectly appropriate for he and his employee to share an after-dinner drink on the way to a charity function. He chose champagne, of course, because there would be champagne at the opera and Hans didn't want to mix drinks and have a headache. Hopefully Annie wouldn't misinterpret the gesture the way Christian apparently did.

Hans stopped in the courtyard and sat down on the black iron bench. It was cold out, but he barely felt it. He couldn't remember ever looking forward to the opera like this.

He folded his arms in front of him and assessed the landscape before him with some satisfaction.

Hills rolled in front of him like a sheet settling over a bed. He owned everything as far as the eye could see. Annie's story about her childhood still haunted him, as he looked over the security that sprawled before him. He had never in his life had a moment of worry about where his next meal was coming from or where he would live in a year or a month or a week. By virtue of his birth, and little else, his future was assured.

As were Besa's and Marta's. At least financially.

Now he understood why Annie felt so strongly about parents being with their children if they could. Her own family had been torn apart by fate, and hadn't been able to be together even though they wanted to be. He could understand why it galled her when she thought people were neglecting their children from sheer laziness, or meanness.

He imagined himself swooping in and helping the young Annie and her mother after her father died. It wasn't the glory of being a hero that would have made it satisfying, he realized. It would be the joy on Annie's face.

He paced the brick courtyard, his breath rising in white drifts around him.

Somewhat uncomfortably, he realized he was beginning to look for that joy in her. As the days passed and he grew accustomed to seeing her, he looked forward to her smile and her laugh. He was even devising ways to bring them out in her. Several times, he'd even rearranged unimportant meetings so he would be available when Annie and the girls were going to be around.

Leo would be outraged if he knew. Already he was on a campaign to get rid of Annie. He thought she was a bad influence on the children. If he'd known of her growing influence over Hans, who knew what he would do?

Not that Hans should worry. He wasn't going to let any feelings for Annie get in the way of her job at the palace and his responsibilities to his country.

He was sure any feelings he had for Annie would pass soon enough.

Chapter Eight

Hans waited for Annie in the reception room, nervously pacing back and forth. He wasn't sure what he was feeling so agitated about, it wasn't as if this event had any more significance than any other. It was probably just the coffee he'd had in the afternoon. Margaret was experimenting with a new coffee roaster and the blends had been quite strong.

His bodyguards waited silently in the hall. He hated the fact that he had to have security trailing him everywhere he went, but it was a necessity. Before his death, Hans's father had taken to keeping six security men with him at all times. If he was leaving the country, even to go to Geneva as Hans was tonight, he might have taken even more.

He heard a noise and looked up. The vision standing in the doorway made Hans's entire body go rigid with desire. "It's time to leave," he said, too brusquely.

"Yes, I know. I—" She had been holding her coat in front of her and she moved it out to the side so he could see her better. "Is this outfit all right?"

It was a slender-fitting black dress that touched just above her knees, revealing a good portion of the stockinged legs he'd admired earlier. There was almost nothing to her outfit, yet it looked surprisingly elegant on her. The only jewelry she wore was a pair of small diamond earrings. Hans recalled a diamond choker that had been his mother's, and thought it would look nice on Annie. But then, anything Annie wore looked good to Hans.

"You look fine," he said, moving to help her on with her coat.

Her shoulders dropped fractionally. "Thanks."

Hans realized he'd understated her beauty, but now that he had he didn't know what else to say without seeming too eager. He didn't want to give her the impression that this was something more than just business.

Christian came into the room, then, his hat clutched before him. "The car is ready, sir."

"Excellent." Hans put a hand on Annie's arm and guided her out to the gleaming, silver Rolls Royce.

"My goodness, I've never traveled in such style!" she exclaimed.

Pleased, Hans said, "It's nothing special." He opened the back door for Annie, instead of waiting for the driver to do it, and she smiled.

"Such chivalry. A girl could get used to this." She corrected herself immediately. "Not that we'll be doing this again or anything." She looked at the plush interior of the car, the buttery leather seats, the dark tinted windows, even a bottle of wine in a silver bucket with ice, and felt a pang.

He closed the door without comment and walked around to the other side. When he got in, he said, "In your country, is such a simple act considered chivalrous?"

She gave a short laugh. "These days it's downright shocking."

The car started slowly out of the courtyard. "American men could perhaps learn a thing or two from European men," Hans said. "That's refreshing."

"American men could learn a *lot,*" she said, smiling. Was that a television in the console? She'd never seen such luxury. She returned her attention to the conversation and tried to hide how bowled over she was by the car. "Your wife lived there for several years. Didn't she tell you how different it was?"

When Hans didn't answer immediately, Annie worried. "Oh, I'm sorry, is that a painful subject?"

"No, no," he said. "I was just trying to recall if she had ever said anything of the kind." He glanced at Annie. "My late wife and I were not very close."

"Oh, I'm sorry."

He gave a shrug. "Nothing to be sorry about. It was a good union."

"That sounds so businesslike."

"It was." He nodded. "There is no other reasonable way to approach it."

"What, marriage?"

"Yes."

"Your marriage was a business transaction?" She sounded surprised.

By this time Hans had lost count of the cultural differences they'd run into. "Of course. My father and Marie's father arranged it when we were young. It was a way of joining our countries and making trade easier between them."

Annie looked shocked. "Did it work?"

He laughed. "Of course. As I said, it was a good union."

She shook her head. "Whatever works for you."

"I wouldn't do it again," he found himself saying, and, worse, watching for her reaction.

She looked at him quickly. "Marry? Or marry for business reasons?"

"Either." He looked at her for a long moment, then took the bottle of champagne from the iced bucket in front of them. "Champagne?"

Her eyes widened and she laughed with pure joy. "Why not?"

They drove through the town in silence as they sipped glasses of yeasty champagne. The holiday lights were up, Hans noticed approvingly. Shopkeepers had decorated their windows. He liked that. It was just the kind of touch that pleased tourists and encouraged them to come back.

As they drove through the inky black night toward Switzerland, they discussed the opera they were about to attend. Hans was pleased to learn that Annie was already familiar with both the story and the composer. If anyone should speak to her afterwards, she would be able to comfortably maintain her side of the conversation.

"There's something I don't understand," Annie said, after they'd been driving for a quarter of an hour or so. "If the point of this mission is to show me the kind of thing you want the children to do, why aren't the children here?"

Greta had asked the same question, damn it, only with Greta there had been raised eyebrows and implications he dared not put to words. "Because," he explained for the second time that day, "they are still a bit young to endure it. Opera appreciation requires a great deal of intellect, and a good deal more life experience than they have at this time. This event was simply a convenient engagement in which to introduce you to my expectations for the children."

"I see." She nodded slowly.

"Yes," he said, nodding himself. Greta had been a bit more difficult to convince. "Once you understand something of what royal life is like, you'll understand better that excursions to town and folk stories about peasants create the wrong idea of what their lives will be like."

"It might benefit them to learn about regular life."

He gave her a cool glance. "It is my wish that the children be prepared for this life, and that is what will happen, with you or without you."

"Point taken."

When Hans looked over at her, he could have sworn he saw a small smile on her lips.

There was a slight delay at the border, and as a result they arrived at the opera house within five

minutes of the curtain. Valuable diplomatic social-
izing time had been lost. Now there was only a brief
period of drinks afterwards during which he could
try to persuade the media darling, Princess Linnea of
Borghdach, to attend an opening gala for the new
Lassberg Ski Resort in January. Her attendance
would guarantee worldwide media coverage and
would probably draw more tourists there than an expensive American television media circus.

Hans left the car under Christian's supervision,
and hurried Annie through the ornate opera house to
the box seats reserved for him. They sat at the very
moment the lights went down. When the music began, he felt himself lulled into a feeling of drowsy
relaxation. Truthfully, it was the most pleasant reaction he'd ever had to the opera. It was a music
form he'd never really enjoyed, but he'd had to endure it so many times he'd gotten used to it.

He studied Annie's profile, lit only by the stage
lights below. She seemed to be enjoying it well
enough. That was good. Perhaps she could cultivate
an appreciation in Besa and Marta. Perhaps they'd
grow to love it so much that they would attend the
functions without him, in his place. The idea appealed to him.

Soon he drifted into other thoughts. Plans for a
proposed government tax cut, a charity that wanted
Marta as patron, the opening of the ski resort which
would undoubtedly bring in much-needed tourism
commerce. He meant to speak with Annie about that,
to get her ideas on keeping tourism going in the summer months.

He was almost sure she'd have something to say on the matter…

When the lights went up, Annie took a moment to wipe the tears from her cheeks before turning to Hans. "That was incredible," she said. "I've never— Sir? Hans?" She touched him but he didn't move, didn't respond.

He was sound asleep.

"Hans," she whispered urgently, grabbing his upper arm and shaking him. She had barely a moment to register how muscular his arm felt before she heard loud voices outside the door. "Wake up!" she whispered again. "Wake up. You fell asleep during the show."

Before she knew what was happening, he'd cupped his hand to the back of her head and drew her to him, her mouth to his. The touch was electric, the kiss irresistible. The moments drew long as their lips mingled, gently exploring, tasting, caressing.

"Hans," she breathed against his mouth.

"Annie." He cupped her face in his hands and kissed her again, this time more deeply.

Annie lost herself in the kiss. Everything about him, the way he tasted, the scent he wore, was different. It was far more intoxicating than any man she'd known before. Was it the supposed superiority of royalty or was there more to it?

The door to the box creaked open. Annie sprang back. "Someone's coming!"

Hans narrowed his eyes. "Annie?" he asked groggily. He straightened in his seat and visibly tried to regain his composure. "I'm sorry, were you saying something?" He frowned and touched a hand to his mouth and she knew, in that moment, that he didn't remember kissing her.

"I was saying," her voice was shaky, "that you must have fallen asleep during the show."

"Good evening, Johann," boomed a rotund, gray-haired gentleman as he made his way slowly into the box. "Why are you hiding here in your seat?"

Hans stood immediately and, Annie had to credit him, he looked as polished as he had when he'd first arrived. "Wolfgang." He gave a short bow, then took Annie's elbow. "Allow me to introduce Anastasia Barimer. Anastasia, this is Wolfgang Fram, one of my late father's dearest friends."

The man's red face beamed. "Anastasia, I'm so very pleased to meet you." He raised an approving eyebrow at Hans. "I haven't heard of this lovely young lady before."

Hans pulled her closer, perhaps to guide her into the hall but they didn't move. "We've only met recently."

"Did you enjoy the opera, Anastasia?"

"Very much." She smiled, but it was more because of the warmth of Hans's hand on her hip, than the pleasure of the music. His kiss still burned on her lips. "It's been a wonderful evening," she said, perhaps a little too breathlessly. From the corner of her eye, she caught Hans's querulous turn of the head.

"I enjoy Duccinia very much," Wolfgang said thoughtfully. "Though I wonder if his work stands up to modern times. I'm glad to hear a young person like yourself is still enjoying it.''

"Oh, I think it absolutely stands up. Puglio's struggle with the devil reminded me very much of the struggles people face in families.'' Her eye was caught by a beautiful blond woman peeking in the door. The minute she noticed her, Hans's hand lifted, leaving a chilly handprint behind.

"Excuse me a moment,'' he said, walking away. "There's someone I have to see.''

Wolfgang took her point about Puglio and ran with it, chatting amiably about the opera's allegory and how it might apply to modern man in the workplace and family home, but Annie could barely pay attention. Her eyes were fixed, instead, on the tall dark Prince of Kublenstein and the willowy platinum blonde, dripping in diamonds, who he was talking with. Their heads were bent close and every once in a while he gave the woman a smile that made Annie's teeth ache.

"Who is that Hans is talking to?'' Wolfgang asked casually. He lifted his monocle to his eye and broke into a wide smile. "Why, it's Linnea! I had no idea she was going to be here tonight, did you?''

"Linnea?'' Annie repeated, frowning.

"Princess Linnea of Borghdach,'' the older man supplied. "I see she's even managed to get in without the press following her.''

The press. Princess Linnea. It was starting to ring a bell. She was famous all over the world, the young widow of an obscure European prince. It seemed to Annie that she'd even seen her on the front of some of the celebrity magazines in the doctor's office. She was beautiful, rich, and titled. A perfect match for Hans. No wonder he'd dashed off the moment he'd seen her.

"Come meet Linnea," Wolfgang urged.

"Oh, no, really—"

"Come, come."

She had no choice but to follow him to where Hans and Linnea seemed positively rapt in conversation. "Hans, dear boy, I don't believe Anastasia and Linnea have met."

Linnea flashed a look at Hans, then smiled. "I don't believe we have," she said, in a lovely precise English accent. "But I was just asking Hans who it was he had brought with him." She held out a hand. "I am delighted to meet you, Anastasia."

Annie shook her hand, then wondered if she should curtsy or something, but decided against it as it would have been overkill. "Very nice to meet you, too, Your Highness."

"Oh, please," she waved a hand airily before her, "call me Linnea."

Reluctantly, Annie added "warm" and "natural" to her mental list of things that made Linnea a perfect catch for Hans.

Linnea was bursting with bubbly energy. "I've got to run, now, Hans, but I'll be glad to go to the resort. That's the fourth, right?"

"The fourth." He nodded. "I'll look forward to seeing you there."

"Wolfgang," she kissed the old man's cheek,

"just wonderful to see you again. Anastasia, I enjoyed meeting you."

Annie smiled, but felt like shrinking when compared to the other woman's larger-than-life vivaciousness. She watched her scoot off, then noticed that every man in the room was also watching her. Except Hans, that was. Hans was looking at Annie, with an expression she was quite sure was pity.

"Are you ready to leave?" he asked cordially.

"Is your work here finished now that Linnea's gone?" Annie asked before she could stop herself. Her face grew hot immediately.

Hans didn't seem to take any notice of her tone at all, though. "Yes. I was hoping to see her tonight and the timing worked out just perfectly. She's coming to the new ski resort opening in January."

"Ah. Good." Annie nodded, as though she understood the significance but she didn't. However, she didn't want him to think she was jealous. Because, of course, she wasn't. "That should be very nice."

"It will be more than nice, it will be outstanding. What a relief." They walked to the coat check and Hans helped Annie on with her coat. "This was certainly a worthwhile evening."

Annie swallowed, but said nothing. She couldn't get her mind off his kiss. What had it meant? Was it all just a mix-up, some kind of dream? But he'd said her name.

They stepped out in the cold and Annie tightened her coat around her. The air had the sweet, metallic scent of snow about it and her spirits lifted.

"Smells like snow," Hans commented, as though reading her thoughts.

This was not the time she wanted him to start reading her thoughts. "Does it? I hadn't noticed." They stopped at the sidewalk and waited for the driver to pull the car up to them. Annie was vaguely aware of Vince and the other bodyguard standing several feet away. They gave her a surprising sense of security.

She and Hans stood side-by-side in silence, white puffs of breath drifting and mingling before them. Like their own souls, Annie thought, then chastised herself for her romanticism. It was just warm breath in cold air, a scientific fact not a romantic symbol.

The car pulled up and the driver opened the door for them. A few minutes after they'd settled into the comfortable back seat, Hans turned to Annie, "When the music ended and you woke me..."

"Yes?"

"Did we..." He stopped, seeming to search for words. Annie had never seen him look at a loss.

She took a short breath. "Did we...?" she prompted.

He glanced at her quickly, catching her gaze and holding it for a moment before looking away. "Did anyone notice? That I'd dozed off, I mean."

She shook her head. "I don't think so."

"Good. Good." He nodded and looked at the fogging window. "It certainly has gotten cold."

He was going to mention the kiss, she just knew it. Why had he stopped. "Hans," she said tentatively.

He turned to her. "Yes?"

She was going to say it. She wasn't going to slide meekly away from the subject, she was going to just confront it head-on. "I enjoyed myself tonight, thank you."

"I'm so glad. Now that you have seen more of what is expected of Besa and Marta, I'm sure you will appreciate that day trips into town are not necessary." He practically scoffed.

The way he said it made it sound like it had been a very silly idea in the first place, and Annie didn't think it had been. "No, following your lead, they just need to learn to sleep upright."

He got it immediately. "That is not the norm, I assure you."

Annie looked at him steadily. "You don't enjoy the opera, do you?"

"That is not the issue."

The car slid onto the smooth highway north. Annie saw a sign that said Lassberg 89 km. That gave them a little more than an hour together before this magical evening ended.

She inhaled deeply. The scent of his aftershave lingered lightly in the cold air. It smelled wonderful, light and so clean it could have been soap.

"I really had fun tonight," Annie said, after they'd driven for half an hour and had exhausted every small talk topic they could think of, including the weather.

"I'm glad to hear it."

"Did you? I mean, do you enjoy doing this kind of thing regularly?"

"It's part of my job."

"So you don't."

"Usually?" He looked at her. "Not particularly."

The car turned the corner and drew into the town square. It was alive with festive lights and Christmas displays, although Christmas was still a month away. With the snow still covering the ground, now painted with brightly colored light, the scene was like something out of a Bing Crosby holiday movie.

After a couple of kilometers passed, Annie said, "It seems to me that being royal means having to spend a lot of time doing things you don't enjoy, things that may even bore you to the point of going to sleep." She gathered her nerve and asked the $64,000 question. "So what do you do when you want to enjoy yourself?"

He took a tight breath, then released it. "I don't have time to enjoy myself."

She tried to laugh but suddenly found herself with a nervous lump in her throat. "Seriously. What do you do just for fun?" He was only inches away. She wanted to reach out and touch him. In fact, she wanted it almost desperately. She crossed her arms in front of her.

He frowned, then shook his head and looked at her. "Nothing comes to mind."

"Come on. When I met you, you were on the train, alone. Sort of incognito. That must be fun, huh?"

"It's work." He cocked his head, as though considering the road before him. "But, yes, I do enjoy it sometimes. That day I met you…"

She caught her breath. "Yes?"

"That was a good day. I'd met a lot of people that morning." He gave a half smile. "Very productive."

Annie smiled to herself. "It's really kind of funny that we met that way, isn't it?"

"You might say it was fate," Hans returned, with a look she couldn't interpret. "If I'm using that word correctly." She wasn't sure what to say. "That almost sounds romantic."

"Indeed," he said softly, still holding her gaze.

Attraction sizzled between them. If he had been an ordinary man—or anyone besides one of the crowned heads of Europe—she would have followed her bold instinct to touch him, perhaps even to kiss him.

But she couldn't. "I would never have imagined who you really were when I first met you."

"I realized that. It was one of the things I liked about you."

She raised an eyebrow. "One of the things? Are there more, Your Highness?"

"Many more." His tone sent shivers down her spine. They were doing a kind of dance, she realized, a little waltz of flirtation and retreat, back and forth. What did he want her to say? What did she want to say?

Then again, maybe she was wrong. Maybe she was flirting and he wasn't, in which case it would be a very grave mistake to say something suggestive.

"I wonder," Hans said slowly. "What you think of me."

Annie searched for an answer. So many things came to mind, most of them inappropriate for an employer-employee relationship, that she was completely stymied.

"Not an easy question, I gather," Hans said after a moment, his mouth curling toward a smile.

"I think a lot of things about you," Annie answered honestly. "You're a wonderful ruler, obviously the people of Kublenstein adore you—"

"And you?"

"Me?" She swallowed.

He edged closer to her, bending in to ask quietly, "How do *you* feel about me?"

His closeness made her dizzy. She felt like Alice once again, falling into the rabbit hole, swirling helplessly amongst incongruous images. "I—I—"

He didn't wait for an answer, instead taking her into his arms and kissing her passionately. She wrapped her arms around him, pulling close, answering him with her kiss.

They drew back, gazing into each other's eyes for a long moment before Annie said, "I guess that's an answer for you."

He looked at her, but somehow it was a distant gaze. "And a question for us both."

Chapter Nine

Leo didn't wait for Greta to let him into Hans's office, he simply burst in, an uncharacteristically bold move for him.

"I understand you took Miss Barimer to the opera last week," he said, as though Hans was a child he'd caught in a lie. "And you never mentioned a word about it to me."

"Yes," Hans replied evenly, trying not to show that he was taken aback by Leo's entrance and vehemence. "Is that a problem for you, Leo?"

"It is a problem. She is a bad influence, not only on your children but apparently now on you yourself."

Hans gave a humorless laugh and leaned back in his chair, lacing his fingers in front of him, tightly, so as to keep from clenching his fists. "A bad influence on me? How did you arrive at that conclusion?"

"She's a crass American, a woman with little to no respect for the traditions of our monarchy. For heaven's sake, she threatened to sue the Lassburg police!" Leo shook his head with disgust. "And now it appears you've fallen under her strange spell."

"You're overreacting," Hans said calmly. "Annie is a good teacher for the children, but that's all she is." Although if that was true, why had Hans spent the rest of the week thinking about his kiss with Annie in the car. If Christian hadn't informed them that they were home, who knows what may have happened. Even now, he kept thinking about unveiling the palace Christmas tree for her to see. It had always been a bit ostentatious to his mind, but others seemed to love it. Annie probably would, too. He wanted to see her face light up with joy when she saw it. But he shouldn't be concerned with that. He tossed the idea aside. He was too busy to bother with such things. Someone else would have to show her the Christmas decorating. "She's only here for the children," he stated firmly.

Leo wasn't giving up. "I only wish that were the truth. I've seen how you look at her. I've heard the change in your voice when she's around, or when her name comes up. You're falling in love with the woman, and her American influence over you could mar the traditions that make this country great."

Hans sat upright. "For one thing, I'm no more in love with that woman than I am with…" He scrambled for a comparison, but there was none. "With anyone else. I'm not in love."

Leo scoffed. "That's what you say."

Hans ignored that. "Second, she does not have undue influence over me and finally, even if she did, I don't believe an American influence is a bad thing for our country."

Leo looked as if Hans had struck him. "I cannot believe my own ears. You're blinded by the woman! We must put a stop to this!" Leo's normally pale face grew pink. "This is my country we're speaking of, my heritage."

"And mine as well." Hans enunciated every word clearly. He stood up slowly, well aware that when he did so, he towered over Leo. "I hope it wasn't your intention to imply that I have any less regard for this country than you do."

Leo's face grew a shade pinker and though he didn't actually take a step back, his posture changed as if he had. "I hope not, sir." He straightened his back. "I fear—but I hope not."

He turned and left the room without another word.

When Leo had gone, Hans sat back down at his desk and replayed the conversation in his head. Leo had never behaved quite like this before. Saying Hans was in love with Annie was...well, it was preposterous. Had Leo lost his hold on reality? Was it the pressure of the end of the year getting to him? Or was he honestly convinced that Annie was some kind of threat to national tradition?

If it hadn't been so deadly serious, Hans would have laughed. Annie, he was reluctant to admit, had made things a little better since she'd arrived. Livelier, at any rate. Not that he was in love with her or anything. It was just a detached observation, things were nicer since Annie had come. They certainly weren't worse or headed in that direction. What was Leo thinking?

And what would he do about it now that Leo had made his disapproval so well known?

"Well?" Hans asked, standing back and looking at Annie. "What do you think?

She looked up at the enormous Christmas tree he indicated. It must have been at least twenty feet tall, and it was trimmed with thousands of tiny white lights and gold bows and ornaments, the intricacy of which was astounding.

"It's breathtaking," she said honestly. "Just the sheer size of it…" She scrambled for something else to say. It looked like something from a magazine or Christmas special on TV. That was the problem. There was no human touch, no handmade ornaments, no treats for the children. It was a grown-up tree, perfect for the kind of living room where no one ever went and where the furniture was covered with plastic protection.

Hans appeared to be waiting for some further comment.

"And the gold," she finished. "Wow."

He frowned, looking closely at her. "You don't like it."

"No, no, it's beautiful, it truly is." Really, in a way it was kind of romantic. It just needed something, some kind of personal touch.

"I don't like it either."

"You don't?"

He shook his head. "I always found it a bit frightening as a child, to tell you the truth."

Annie laughed. "Frightening?"

He smiled, too. "Look at it. If that fell over on you, you'd have little chance of getting out unharmed."

She laughed even harder. "Yes, I suppose that's true." She shook her head, sobering. "Why do you have the tree if you don't like it?"

He shrugged. "Tradition. They've brought it in one week before Christmas every single year. It's always looked like that and it's always been right here in the entry hall."

She looked again. "It does fit perfectly in that space. With all those tall windows, it's probably very pretty from outside."

"Mmm."

She continued to consider the tree and the children. "Do the children get to put any of their own decorations on this one?"

"They don't have any decorations of their own," Hans said, looking baffled at the idea.

"Not even candy canes?"

"No."

The idea was foreign to her. "And they don't make anything? Pinecones? Popcorn strings?"

Hans looked from Annie to the tree and back. "Can you imagine strings of popcorn on this tree?"

She couldn't. But she could imagine a smaller tree in the nursery, loaded with handmade ornaments and toys. "Perhaps we should make another tree for the children, up in the nursery. Something a little less...daunting.''

Hans dismissed the idea with a wave of his hand. ''It's unnecessary. I'm quite sure they like this one.'' An invisible wall went up between them.

''Oh, I'm sure they do. Just as you did as a child. I just thought they might enjoy doing some of their own handiwork.''

He gave a half shrug. ''If you like. Barnes, the gardener, can bring a small tree in for you.''

''Would you like to help decorate it?''

He gave her a withering look. ''No. Thank you.''

For a moment she was hurt, but something told her that his coldness wasn't meant for her. ''Will you come see it when it's done?''

She was right. The wall went down very slightly. Hans said, ''I have a feeling I'll get an argument if I say no.''

''You will.''

He walked over to her and stopped directly before her. ''Then we'll see.''

She took a shaking breath and kept her arms firmly at her sides. ''Can we get more of a commitment than that, Your Highness?''

He touched her cheek. ''No.'' Then he smiled and walked past her, back in the direction of his office. ''It's time for you to get the girls.''

She looked at her watch and saw that it was, indeed, the end of the school day for them. ''Thanks for showing me the tree,'' she called, lamely, after him.

He raised a hand but didn't look back. "You're welcome."

"I'll let you know when the other one is ready."

"I'm sure you will." He disappeared around the corner.

Annie stood for a moment, watching where he'd gone. Then she raised a finger to her cheek where he'd touched her. "I will," she said softly, recalling—for the hundredth time—his kiss in the car.

Just as Hans had said, Barnes was quick to get a four-and-a-half-foot evergreen into the nursery. It arrived early the next morning, which was Saturday. Besa and Marta watched in amazement as the little tree was brought in, set up, and left just for them.

"What will we do with it?" Marta asked eagerly.

"You two are going to decorate it."

"We are?" Besa asked, looking genuinely puzzled.

"Yep."

"Like the one downstairs?"

"Not quite. This one will look different because it'll be your very own. You can put anything you want on it. But I do have some suggestions."

They spent the better part of the morning, wandering around the grounds picking up odds and ends that they could use for decorating the tree. Annie had managed to get Margaret to pop some corn, and she even found some candy canes in the kitchen. The housekeeper helped by gathering a small sewing basket with yarn and scraps of fabric.

By mid-afternoon, a good percentage of the staff

had stopped by the nursery with contributions or suggestions for how they'd done things when they were
children. The day took on a festive air that Annie
then realized had been lacking in the palace, especially considering that Christmas was seven days
away.

Margaret came up to help when she'd finished her
duties in the kitchen. She put the finishing touches
on the candy cane stick horses and held Besa up as
she put them on the higher branches.

When they had finished, the tree was charming. It
was a far different tree than the one downstairs. It
wasn't grand by any definition, but in its own way
it stood up to the comparison fairly well.

"It's a noble little tree," Margaret pointed out.

"Yes, it is," Annie agreed, smiling at the cheerful
haven they'd turned the nursery into. "I can't wait
for Prince Johann to see it."

Margaret looked at her open-mouthed. "You're
joking, aren't you?"

"No. Why?"

Margaret's features turned dramatic. She looked
for Besa and Marta, who were playing across the
room, then whispered to Annie, "He hates Christmas, that one does."

"Oh, come on. Why would he hate Christmas?"

"I don't know," Margaret said in a stage whisper,
"but every year during this season he mopes around
something awful. And temper…well! We can't wait
until the new year has come and gone so we can get
back to normal."

"It's true," Marta said, having heard Margaret. "Papa doesn't like Christmas."

Annie flashed Margaret a look of recrimination. "Marta, I'm sure it's not that your father doesn't like Christmas. He's probably just very busy this time of year."

Marta sighed and shook her head, a gesture far too old for her years. "I don't think so."

Annie was thoughtful. Why would Hans hate Christmas? One would imagine that the ruler of a country would be at his absolute happiest during the holiday season. She remembered his story about the Christmas tree, how he'd never liked it. Clearly he'd had some troubles as a boy which hadn't been helped. She couldn't stop herself from wondering if she could help now. If anything could change his mind about the holidays, it would be his children. When he saw how joyful they were, he'd feel the same way himself. "Well," she said, with new resolve. "Then we'll just have to change his mind."

Three days left. In three days it would be Christmas Eve, the night of the annual masquerade ball at the palace. A night he dreaded every year. The night that was presented to the world as a time for family and love had always meant a dizzying round of parties for his parents and nannies for him. Hans felt it was the coldest night of the year. But just one week after that, Kublenstein would have rung in the new year in its usual over-the-top fashion and then it would be over for another year.

Hans couldn't wait.

He was on his way to the dining room for dinner. As he passed the ornate tree in the hallway he smiled to himself, thinking of Annie's reaction to it. It was kind of charming that she wanted to decorate a small tree herself, rather than enjoy this enormous, expensive monstrosity that was already up. Since she'd made the request, he'd seen very little of her or his daughters. Most of their interaction at the dinner table had been punctuated with secretive glances and giggles between the girls.

This night he'd had just about enough of it. "I can't help but get the impression," he said, over coq au vin, "that the three of you are up to something."

Immediately Besa and Marta sat up straight and looked at him with faces painted with innocence.

"We're being good," Besa said in a tiny voice.

"Where Miss Barimer is concerned," he said, without taking his eyes off her, "I have learned to be cautious." He smiled, but barely.

"Understood," she said to him. Then to the girls, "I think it's time we showed your father what we've been working on, don't you?"

"Can we?" Marta asked. "Is it ready yet?"

Annie smiled. "I think so."

Hans eyed Annie suspiciously. "And what is it?"

"Well, several things, as a matter of fact."

"Can we show him now?" Besa asked, jumping up from her chair.

"Sit," Hans said sharply. "You are not excused from the table until you have finished your dinner. As you well know."

Besa sat, but within moments her face started to crumple and her eyes filled with tears. Hans felt sorry for her unhappiness, but she had to remember her place.

Annie reached over and touched Besa's arm. "I know you're eager to show him, honey, but it can wait a few more minutes, can't it?"

"Y-yes." Besa sniffled convulsively.

"Good girl, then. Eat your dinner."

Hans watched the exchange with feelings he couldn't quite identify. Part of him wished he'd had the same gentle treatment as a child, but part of him railed at Annie's softness in a situation that traditionally needed firmness. After all, the girls had to learn to keep in control and do what was expected of them the first time. There were no second chances on the public stage.

Then again, maybe the balance of Annie's gentleness and his firmness would have more of an impact on the children than either one of them would alone.

That was nonsense, he told himself right away. He'd done fine for years before Annie had come along. It wasn't as if he couldn't do without her now.

"Miss Barimer," he said in a hard voice.

She drew her hand back from Besa, startled, and turned to Hans. "Yes?"

That was enough. The situation was back under his control. Hans felt a small measure of relief and smiled wanly. "Please pass the salt."

The scene at dinner continued to trouble Hans long after he'd left the table, though he wasn't sure why.

He was right, he was absolutely certain of it. How had Annie made him doubt that? How could she have come into his life and, within mere weeks, actually caused him to doubt almost everything he'd held true his whole life.

When he'd grown up, a child had been treated as a child, not as an adult. Childish outbursts had been met with icy reserve, not compassion. Compassion would only encourage more outbursts, wouldn't it? He frowned. Maybe. On the other hand, maybe he would have benefited from the understanding that his feelings mattered as a child. Maybe it wouldn't have been such a lonely life.

Then again, maybe if he'd been coddled that way he wouldn't be such an effective leader now. Most of the Crowned Heads of Europe were figureheads, with no governmental power at all. Hans, on the other hand, had been widely praised as an intelligent ruler, smoothly bringing his country through the economic and political hard times that had begun after the Second World War during his father's reign and continued right on through until his father's death five years ago.

Now Annie was making him doubt himself.

Only a voice in him said maybe it wasn't that Annie had made him do anything, but that she'd opened his eyes to the possibility that the way he'd been raised wasn't necessarily the best way.

The thought made him extremely uncomfortable.

There was a discreet knock at the door to the library where he was sitting, and a maid entered, carrying a piece of paper. She handed it to him, said, "From the Princesses Besa and Marta," then gave a slight bow and left.

He waited until she'd closed the door behind her before looking at the folded colored paper. It was green, shaped something like a fir tree, with red and yellow cut-out circles glued to it. Inside, Marta had written, in a careful hand, Please come to the nursery for a surprise.

He stared at the paper for a minute, then sighed. A surprise. He dropped the paper on the table next to where he'd been sitting and walked alone through the empty halls and stairways to the nursery.

When he arrived upstairs, the noise on the other side of the nursery door was enough to rouse the dead. Shrieks of laughter were punctuated with hurried instructions to put this here or put that there and loud shushes. He couldn't help smiling as he listened.

Finally he knocked.

"Wait, wait, wait, he's here," he heard Annie say in a loud stage whisper. "Get ready."

There was a confusion of footsteps, then Besa called, "Come in!"

Hans opened the door. The lights were dimmed so that the first thing he saw was an odd-shaped little fir tree, covered in homemade paper ornaments, strings of popcorn, a few things he couldn't quite identify, and strings of colored lights like the shops in town had outside. It was quite a sight. He had to admit, although not out loud, that it was the most cheerful symbol of the holidays that he'd ever seen. Perhaps his lifelong perception of Christmas as a time of loneliness could change.

A tape player in the corner jingled softly with an American singer singing Christmas carols.

"What do you think of it?" Marta asked.

"Isn't it pretty?" Besa added.

He looked at Annie, standing in the candlelike glow, and said, "Yes. Very pretty." The desire to go to her and take her in his arms, to lose himself in her warm embrace, was so strong it hurt.

Annie didn't move, didn't flinch or look down shyly, the way he might have expected. She met his gaze with strength he could nearly feel. "It's all for you," she said, then took a short breath. "We wanted you to enjoy Christmas this year."

"Quite ambitious of you."

She cocked her head. "Maybe, but I figure if I make things different from usual, you've got a better shot."

"This is definitely different," he answered, his eye skimming over the little tree.

"So it's a start," Annie ventured with half a smile.

He looked at her for a moment, then gave a single nod. "It's a start."

"We have things for you," Besa cried, apparently tired of the low-key conversation. She ran to some tissue-covered gifts under the tree, and carried them back to Hans. First she handed him a white one with a huge flopping bow. "This one's from me," she said proudly.

"From you, eh? Let's see what it is." He chuckled and tore the paper back. There was a pinecone, painted a shining—if uneven—gold. "That's very nice, Besa, did you do it yourself?"

She nodded eagerly.

"Very good work. Thank you."

"You're welcome." She handed him the other package. "This is Marta's."

"I made it myself, too, Papa."

For a moment, he wished he could just freeze time. He couldn't remember ever having seen his girls so relaxed and happy, not even when Marie was still alive. The coziness Annie had created, and the speed with which she'd achieved it, was breathtaking.

Not that it was going to turn him into a fan of the holidays, of course. But she'd warmed it up considerably for his daughters and for that he was immeasurably grateful. She'd achieved something he never could have.

He set the pinecone down and opened the larger package. At first he didn't know what it was, it looked like a bundle of sticks. But when he took all the paper away and looked closer he saw it was a twig frame around a picture of Besa and Marta outside in the woods.

"Do you like it?" Marta asked quietly.

He smiled. "Very much. It's lovely." He bent down and held his arms out to his daughters. They rushed into him, giggling and kissing his cheeks.

He felt Annie's watchful gaze on him from across the room. When he stood up, she was smiling.

"So maybe Christmas isn't entirely bad after all?" she said lightly.

"Not entirely, no," he conceded. "But then, we still have several days to go."

Annie laughed. "You're a real Scrooge, you know that?"

"Then I'm in the holiday spirit." He smiled.

"Is Annie going to the masquerade ball?" Marta asked her father.

"No, Marta—" Annie began, but Hans interrupted her.

"If she likes," he said.

"It's on Christmas Eve," Marta explained to Annie. "Everyone wears a mask, so you don't know who they are, and you may ask three questions in order to determine their identity. I can't wait until I'm old enough to go," she added dreamily.

Annie felt Hans's eyes on her as she said, "Well, since you are not old enough, and I'm in charge of you, I'll be spending the evening with you." She looked at Hans and felt her face grow warm. "You'll have to tell us all about it afterward."

He gave a nod. "As you wish."

Besa tugged at Annie's sweater. "Can we go get the hot chocolate now?"

Annie was grateful for the interruption. "That's right, I nearly forgot. Margaret should have it ready by now. You two run on down and get it, okay?"

When the girls had scurried off, Hans said, "You went to a lot of trouble to do this for them. Thank you."

"It wasn't just for them," she answered, her eyes steadily upon him.

His breath tightened. "Meaning…?"

"I wanted to do it for you, too." She gave an embarrassed smile and looked down for a moment, before adding, "Maybe I shouldn't admit that, but it's true."

He took several steps toward her, stopping close. "For me," he repeated, bemused by what she'd said. "I'm not sure anyone's ever taken such measures before." He said it frankly, without a hint of self-pity.

"All the more reason to do it," Annie said, with a light shrug.

"No." He put his hands on her shoulders and looked deeply into her eyes. His intention was to tell her not to bother with him, to worry about the children instead, but when she looked up at him, her blue eyes almost liquid with compassion, he couldn't stop himself. He kissed her. Hard at first—urgent, angry, desperate, then softer, with all the longing he'd felt for her for so long. She roused every emotion in him and painted them all with desire.

He twined his fingers in her hair, clutching almost desperately. He wanted her like he'd never wanted any woman before. It wasn't merely physical, it was spiritual. He wanted her presence in his life, in his home, forever.

"Hans," she murmured against his mouth, wrapping her arms around him and holding on tight.

He kissed her deeply, then embraced her, lowering

his mouth to her neck and shoulder. "I'm sorry," he said, in German. "We shouldn't be doing this." But he couldn't let her go.

"Why not?" Annie asked weakly, trailing her hands up and down his back. "It feels right."

"You don't want to get involved with me." He pulled back then, and eyed her sternly. "We must stop this."

"I want to start it," she said, persuading him with a guileless look.

So did he. More than anything, so did he. "You don't want this life."

"I don't?" She raised an eyebrow. "Or you don't?"

"Perhaps neither of us should, but for me there is no choice. You would be happier with a different man, a man with a less complicated existence."

"How does one choose who one falls in love with?"

It felt like she'd punched him in the stomach. "Are you...in love?"

For a long moment, she didn't answer. Her eyes were filled with tears.

He kissed her again, hard, then pushed away from her. "It's impossible."

"Why? Don't you feel anything for me?"

Faced with the question, he trembled at how much he felt for her. "What I feel isn't the issue," he evaded.

She took his hands in hers. "What do you feel?"

"As I said—"

She squeezed. *"What do you feel?"*

He was saved from answering by the return of Besa and Marta. However, he and Annie were still face-to-face, holding hands, when they entered. Obviously this was far more interesting than the snack they'd planned, and they clattered the cups of hot chocolate down on the table.

"Are you two getting married?" Besa asked instantly, her eyes alight.

"No, no, Besa," Annie started, going to the child. "We were just having a talk."

"It looked like you were kissing," she said, then giggled.

"Did it?" Annie said, with an attempt at a laugh.

"Yes, and that's what people do when they get married. If you got married you'd be our mother."

Marta watched the exchange silently. Hans watched her.

"Whoa, wait a minute, little princess, no one said anything about getting married." Annie shot Hans an imploring look.

"What did you bring up?" he asked, aware that Marta's even gaze had turned to him.

"We'd like to have a new mother," Marta said to him quietly.

Struck by her statement, he froze for a moment, then ruffled her hair. "That's why we have Annie here." Though he was trying to make light of the situation, there was a heaviness to his heart that he couldn't hide.

That's why they had Annie.

"Come on," Annie interrupted, picking up the hot mugs of chocolate. "Everybody gets one." She handed one to Hans and their fingers bumped as he took it. Their eyes met, but he looked away.

When everyone had a mug, Annie raised hers in the air. "To a Merry Christmas," she said brightly. "And a happy new year."

Chapter Ten

"Thank you for coming so promptly, Miss Barimer," Leo said with a smugness that made Annie's skin crawl. It was Christmas Eve, and he'd called her to his office on an "emergency." She'd gone with a great amount of trepidation.

He studied the intercom on his desk, pushing several buttons and calling for Greta until he finally pushed the right one and she answered. He said to her, "I want absolutely no interruptions while I'm meeting with Miss Barimer."

Annie's stomach turned into a knot.

He turned back to her. "I'll get directly to the point. The newspaper has sent me an advance copy of tomorrow's lead story. I'm afraid this will be quite the upsetting Christmas Eve gift for His Highness." He took a large manilla envelope from the side drawer of his desk and slid it across to her. "Go ahead. Take a look."

She took the envelope and opened it carefully. The front page was monopolized by a photo of Hans and Annie at the opera, kissing in the box after the curtain went down. The headline was in bold capital letters: Nanny Strikes Gold as Mistress of the Prince.

Annie dropped the envelope on the desk and recoiled in horror. "That's not true!"

Leo's mouth formed a self-satisfied line. "It certainly looks true."

"It's not!" She felt the blood drain from her face and tingle down into her toes. "Where would they get such an idea?" As soon as she asked, she knew the answer was obvious.

"The question," Leo said with deliberate slowness, "is what are we going to do about it. I'm afraid the only option is for you to leave and leave quietly. Prince Johann does not need this kind of publicity."

Annie's throat tightened. "I never meant—"

"Whether you meant to or not, Miss Barimer, you have created problems repeatedly, ever since you arrived."

She couldn't speak.

"So if you would be so good as to pack your things, I will tell His Highness why you are leaving."

The door burst open with the force of a bomb.

Annie jerked around to see Hans standing there, glowering at the two of them. Whatever emotion had driven him this far also made him seem ten feet tall, and Annie had a sense of Leo shrinking back from him. She, on the other hand, had to fight the urge to run to Hans for safety.

Hans stormed over to Leo's desk and slapped a

hand down on the intercom. "You really should learn to turn your speaker off, Leo, I could hear you all the way in my office."

"You…heard?" Leo asked, cowering back.

"I did. Now," he turned to Annie, "if Miss Barimer is leaving," his voice grew low, and too calm. "I'd like to hear it from her."

"Look, I'm not sure what—" Annie began.

Leo shuffled over between the two of them. "I don't like to have to show you this, sir, but I don't see what choice I have. Tomorrow it will be out anyway." He handed the envelope to Hans as carefully as if it were made of gold leaf.

Hans snatched it from him. "What is this?" he asked, opening it and pulling out the newspaper. When he looked at the front page, his brow lowered and his eyes appeared to grow very dark. "What the hell is this?"

"It is, I'm afraid, the kind of thing I've been warning you about, sir," Leo answered placidly. Clearly he felt some point of his was being made.

Hans shook his head and began pacing before them, tapping the envelope against his leg. "It's untrue," he argued. "This is against the law. I'll contact my attorney, and then I'll contact the editor of the paper. I've known him for years. You would have thought he'd know better."

"It's not against the law if it's true," Leo said twisting his hands in front of him.

"It's not true!" Hans thundered. He held the paper up again. "Obviously this is some kind of doctored photo."

Annie felt the blood rise to her face again, burning mercilessly. "Actually, it's probably not."

Silence fell as two sets of eyes turned to her.

"See?" Leo said triumphantly, returning to his place behind the desk. "She probably set the whole thing up. She's a gold digger. I knew she was the wrong type of person from the start."

Hans ignored him and kept his gaze on her. "What do you mean it's not? You can see for yourself that it looks like we're...we're in a compromising position."

She tried to take a deep breath, but it was like breathing underwater. She glanced nervously at Leo then back at Hans. "After the curtain came down that night," she started quietly. "I noticed you were dozing. I went to wake you up and..." She swallowed and gestured at the paper. "That's what happened."

Something in Hans's face softened. "You kissed me?"

Her face grew warmer. "Actually you kissed me."

Their eyes lingered on each other for a long, delicious moment, and she could almost imagine this to be a private exchange.

"Perhaps you were too influenced by the fairy tale of Sleeping Beauty, Miss Barimer," Leo said behind her, reminding her just how unromantic this moment was. There was ugly superiority in his tone. "There are better ways to wake the prince."

"Enough!" Hans barked, stepping away from Annie and closer to the desk. He pointed a finger at

Leo. "I've heard enough from you. Please leave us alone."

"Sir, you're in my office—"

"And you are in my home," Hans said evenly.

Annie felt a lump of emotion rise in her throat and burn in her eyes, but she made an effort to keep silent. After all, there was something happening between the two men that she didn't understand, and it was best not to make it worse.

"Sir," Leo said again, now in a different voice. She could tell he was going for diplomacy. "I realize that you are somewhat blind to Miss Barimer's tricks, but it's obvious from where I stand that she's behind the publication of these pictures."

"Me?" She found her voice again.

"To what end?" Hans asked.

Leo raised his eyebrows. "I believe she is trying to trap you into a more personal relationship."

"Trap him?" Annie repeated, incredulous. "You think I'm trying to trap the Prince of Kublenstein into a relationship by having these kinds of pictures and tawdry insinuations published in the newspaper? That's crazy."

"Perhaps," Leo said coolly. "Perhaps not."

"How foolish would I have to be to even try something like that? Obviously the newspaper can reveal who gave them the story."

Leo's face lost a shade of color. "It's not necessary to delve into that. Even if you weren't the one who gave it to them, the fact remains that this kind of publicity is following you all around the country and you're turning the monarchy into a bad joke."

He turned to Hans. "Your father would never have let this happen."

Hans straightened to his full, regal height. "And that's the problem, isn't it, Leo? I am not my father. That is something you have regretted since he died."

"He was a great man," Leo said, with touching emotion.

"Yes, he was," Hans said, a little more gently. "But he's gone now and I cannot be him, especially not to please you and a small portion of old-school thinking men who prefer to run the government as a nineteenth-century monarchy. Times have changed, Leo. I suggest you do the same."

"I will not!"

Hans stepped closer to Annie, draping her in his protective presence. "I'm sorry you feel that way, Leo. Under the circumstances, I feel compelled to accept your resignation."

Leo looked stricken. "My—Sir, you must be confused. She—she's trying to trap you."

"She doesn't need to trap me," Hans said.

Annie caught her breath. What did he mean?

"I cannot listen to this," Leo said, making his way out from behind his desk. He stopped at the doorway and turned back to them, his face red. "Thank goodness your father isn't here to see this."

"Indeed."

This seemed to outrage Leo further, and he sputtered a few ill-chosen words and left.

Hans shook his head, then turned to Annie and took her hands in his. "I'm sorry you had to go through all of this."

She shrugged her trembling shoulders. "Leo is of the old school, just like you said. I'm sure he meant well. Somehow."

"His actions could have been devastating."

She pressed her lips together and swallowed. "Well, it's not your fault."

He looked at her and the corner of his mouth turned up. "That's something I don't often hear you say."

The door opened. "Sir," Greta said gently. "The editor of the newspaper, Herr Lennon, is on the line. It seems he has some information about an informant in the palace."

Hans straightened, but kept a hand on Annie's back. She felt tension in his touch which hadn't been there a moment before. "Does he know who?"

Greta nodded. "I'm afraid so."

"Well? Who is it?"

"Herr Kolbort, sir."

Hans nodded. "I see." He turned to Annie and said, with resignation, "Excuse me. I'd like to have this behind me before the ball tonight."

Annie had never in her life been so close to anything as grand as a ball. The excitement had built in the palace all day long, with the busy voices of the staff and the sporadic rehearsal of the orchestra, everything was coming together for one huge event.

And now it was here.

The high notes of string instruments rose into the air and wound through the stairway to the hallway where Besa, Marta, and Annie were perched, watching the guests enter the palace. Women were draped in jewels, gloves, and furs, men wore black tie and tails, and all of them disguised their faces with masks. Some guests were clearly recognizable to those who knew them, others were so cleverly and subtly disguised that even their own mothers might not have known them.

"That's the Duchess Rothmore," Marta whispered, pointing to a portly woman with blond hair piled high atop her head. "Her hair is usually as black as coal but I'd know her figure anywhere."

Besa giggled, then cried, "And there's Princess Linnea!" so loud they had to shush her.

"Papa was hoping she'd come this year," Marta said knowingly.

Annie wanted to ask what she meant, but bit her tongue.

"Where is Papa?" Besa asked next, in a very loud whisper.

"I don't know, I haven't seen him yet," Marta replied. "He's usually hard to spot, though. Have you seen him, Miss Barimer?"

"No, I haven't." Though heaven knew she'd been looking.

"Miss Barimer," a woman's voice said behind them.

Annie jumped, and turned to see Greta standing there in an elegant blue ball gown, and a long blond wig. Annie's face grew hot as she realized Greta knew she'd been spying with the children. "We just wanted to see what it was like," she said with a small laugh.

Greta smiled warmly. "There are better vantage points. For example, the ballroom floor."

"Papa said you could go if you wanted to," Marta pointed out, excitedly.

A tiny thread of excitement wound through Annie, but she kept it at bay. "He said that to be polite, honey."

"To the contrary, Miss Barimer," Greta said, a knowing look on her face. "I believe he's looking for you."

"But I told him I wasn't coming."

"I know. He told me so when I asked. Still, I believe he is hoping."

Greta smiled. "Margaret is in the nursery, waiting to put the children to bed. I'm here to help you get dressed for the ball."

Excitement grew in Annie. "But—this is crazy. Isn't it? I don't even have anything to wear!"

"Not to worry. I have two dresses laid out on your bed for you to choose from."

"My goodness, you're just like a fairy god-mother."

"Perhaps. Only you don't need magic this evening, you need only to be yourself."

The girls giggled and made their own Cinderella jokes.

"Daddy's just like the prince," Besa said, charmingly missing the reality of her statement.

Annie raised a hand to her lips. He was, indeed, a Prince Charming to her. She was afraid to give in to the fantasy, for fear it would disappear in her hands. "Are you sure I should do this?"

Greta nodded and took Annie's arm to usher her into her room. ''Prince Johann is a secretive man. I cannot say I can read his mind, but I strongly believe he will welcome you most warmly.''

Just half an hour later, a visibly nervous Annie stepped down the grand stairway in a shimmering gold gown, with golden shoes that fit her perfectly, a pale blond wig, and a golden mask which completely hid her identity. That anonymity was the only thing that kept her from running back to her room in terror and closing the door behind her. There were so many questions that could have stopped her from going downstairs. Did Hans really want her there? Was it appropriate for someone in her position to attend? Greta assured her it was, and, indeed, the fact that Greta was a regular guest gave Annie some comfort.

What she really feared was that she was wearing her heart on her sleeve, or at least the long white gloves that went with her gown, and that Hans would see it and be horrified at it. She couldn't help that, she decided. She'd never been good at hiding her feelings. He was bound to realize them someday, if he didn't already.

''You look lovely,'' Greta said, when they stood at the door to the ballroom.

It was more incredible than Annie had ever imagined. The ceiling was impossibly high, with ornately gilded walls and arched buttresses overhead. At the far end of the room, two sets of glass doors showed a vista of glittering holiday lights, adorning all the trees in the garden surrounding the palace. The music sang sweetly around the room, like a kindly spirit, and the guests smiled and laughed, and drank golden champagne from tall fluted glasses.

"I'm really out of place here," Annie whispered to Greta.

Greta looked at her. "Do you really feel that? Or do you just think it?"

Annie considered before answering. The truth was, her nervousness was dissolving. It was only a small voice in her mind that said she didn't belong. Her heart said she did. She smiled at Greta. "You're right. I'm talking myself out of this when I really want nothing more than to be right here."

"I suspected as much," Greta said. "Now, do you know the three questions rule?"

"The girls mentioned it. You get to ask three questions to figure out who you're talking to?"

Greta nodded. "Yes, three questions that can be answered with a yes or a no." She took Annie's hand and gave it a quick squeeze. "I'm going to leave you now, lest my presence gives you away. Have fun!"

"Thank you," Annie said, and watched Greta sweep off in a cloud of blue chiffon.

Almost immediately, a stout man with a mustache and Zorro-style black mask approached her. "Good evening," he said in German. "May I have this dance?"

Annie hesitated for only a moment, then smiled. She was going to devour every precious moment of this evening. "I'd be honored," she said, and together they went to the dance floor.

It was from there, as they turned wide waltzing circles to the Blue Danube, that she spotted Hans in the far corner. Though his black mask covered his entire face, and a top hat covered his wonderful dark hair, she knew him immediately by his posture and the way he held himself. Judging from the fact that he was alone, though, she guessed that others didn't know his identity as easily.

The music ended and there was a ripple of applause.

"Thank you very much," Annie said, excusing herself.

"Wait," her dance partner objected. "Three questions."

She stopped. What the heck? "Go ahead," she said, with a light smile.

"Were you born in Kublenstein?"

This was easy. "No."

"Germany?"

She gave a light laugh. "No."

"Have you been to this ball before?"

She shook her head. "No, I haven't."

He hesitated then snapped his fingers. "You are the Duchess of Rothmore's niece!"

"Sorry, no," she smiled. She'd never enjoyed herself so much in her life. The only thing that could make it better—infinitely better—was being with Hans. "But thank you for the dance."

She left and hurried through the crowd to where Hans had been standing only moments before but he was gone. Something inside of her deflated. She'd missed the perfect opportunity to talk with him with no one else around. By now he'd probably been snagged by some beautiful aristocrat, probably Princess Linnea, who had him in her clutches. She looked to the dance floor, scanning the beautiful dancers with something that felt a lot like dread.

"Are you looking for someone?" a familiar voice behind her asked.

She turned back, and it was him. Yet he was even less recognizable up close than he had been from a distance. The mask covered his face entirely, and the incredible green eyes that she knew were there someplace were not easily distinguished from behind the mask.

"Just admiring the dancers," she said in her very best German. She didn't want to give herself away with her accent.

"Care to join them, Miss…?" he asked, extending a white-gloved hand.

So he didn't know who she was! A thrill ran through her. "Thank you," she said, taking his hand and walking out to the floor with him.

It was a slow dance this time, but her close proximity to Hans left her far more breathless than the energetic waltz had.

"Are you enjoying yourself this evening, Miss…?"

She loved this game. "Very much. Are you, Mr…?"

He adjusted his grip around her waist, inadvertently pulling her closer. "More than usual."

She took a tight breath. "Why is that?"

He paused before answering. "Because I have recently met the woman I want to marry, and she is here tonight.''

Annie's chest tightened. For a wild moment, she thought perhaps she was wrong about this being Hans, but she wasn't. She knew it was him. And he didn't know it was her. In fact, he didn't expect her to come at all, which meant that he was talking about someone else.

She remembered Besa's exclamation that Princess Linnea had arrived, and that Hans was hoping she would. Annie's heart sank.

''Does she know of your intentions?'' she asked, her voice shaking.

He gave a single nod. ''I believe so. What I don't know is how she will respond.''

Suddenly Annie felt foolish in her fancy dress and preposterous wig. They had only given her the means to eavesdrop on a conversation she didn't want to hear.

''It's a very romantic setting for a proposal,'' she said, trying to keep her voice steady.

''I hope she agrees. You see, I'm afraid she may be tired of the setting.''

That clinched it, everyone knew Linnea was an adventurer who probably didn't want to be tied down in one place. She'd been photographed all over the world. But had he met her only recently?

''Many couples have to work that kind of thing out,'' Annie replied, wishing she could curl up in a ball and roll away.

''Sadly we don't have that kind of flexibility. We

must live in Kublenstein, and I fear she won't want to. It would require giving up her own nationality."

"You know what they say," Annie said, no longer trying so hard to disguise her American accent. "Love conquers all."

How had this happened? Only a few nights ago Hans had told her he didn't intend to marry again for any reason. He'd been quite clear on that point. What had happened to that?

How could Greta have encouraged her to come down here when Hans was about to propose to Princess Linnea?

Then again, Greta hadn't made any promises to Annie. In fact, she hadn't exactly said that Hans wanted Annie there for personal reasons. Maybe Annie had misread the entire conversation.

"Interesting that you should say that," Hans said. "Because I didn't believe that such a proposal required love until recently. A very wise woman made me see that."

That, she knew, was a reference to herself. "Not that wise."

"I beg your pardon?"

She gathered her wits. "I mean, most people feel marriage is a romantic proposition. It doesn't take a lot of wisdom. In fact, maybe it's not so wise at all."

He laughed. "You may be correct. But falling in love can take you by surprise."

"I certainly agree with that." Her chest ached. The large ballroom was beginning to feel small and suffocating.

The music ended, mercifully, and Annie clapped

politely for a moment before saying, "Excuse me, please."

She turned to go, but Hans caught her arm.

"Wait a moment, I get to ask you three questions and guess your identity."

She took a short breath to keep her emotions under control. "I'm sorry, but there's something I must do."

"You're here for the ball, aren't you?"

She didn't want him to know it was her, if he didn't already. That would only further her humiliation. Instead she had to play the part. "I am," she said, her shoulders sagging. "Ask your questions."

He took her hand and led her off the dance floor to stand by the tall glass doors. "One. Do you like living in Lassberg?"

She swallowed. "How do you know I live in Lassberg?"

He shrugged. "If you don't, then I suppose the answer is no."

Apprehension crept over her skin. He knew it was her. "I like it, yes."

"Ah. Good. Next question. Are you able to stay long? Perhaps indefinitely?"

He did know it was her! He knew and he wanted her to stay on and take care of the children once he was married to Linnea! As much as she loved Besa and Marta she wasn't sure she could stand the pain of living here under those circumstances.

"I don't know," she said, in a voice that barely held the weight of her words. Tears burned in her eyes. "Please excuse me, I really can't wait any longer. I'm sorry." She turned and hurried from the room without waiting for his response.

She rushed up the stairs and into the quiet solitude of her room. As soon as she'd closed the door behind her, she threw off the mask and wiped the foolish tears from her cheeks. What was she crying for? She'd fallen in love with a prince, for Pete's sake, she should have known nothing could ever come of it. This was no different than having a crush on a rock singer or movie star. She'd never cried because Mel Gibson was taken.

There was a knock on the door. Greta, she figured. She'd probably seen her running away and wanted to know what was wrong. She checked her image in the mirror as she passed, wiped a bit of mascara from under her left eye, took a deep breath and opened the door.

It wasn't Greta.

It was Hans. Minus the mask and the hat.

"You didn't let me ask my third question," he said softly, his gaze penetrating. He radiated confidence.

"So you did know it was me," Annie said dully.

He gave a short laugh. "Neither one of us is the master of disguise we believed ourselves to be."

She had to smile at that. "So my next job won't be as an actress."

"I was hoping you wouldn't have a next job."

She sighed. "I can't think about that right now." She sniffed. "Don't you have to talk to Linnea?"

"Linnea? I haven't even seen her this evening."

Annie was shocked. "You haven't?"

He shook his head. "Though I wasn't particularly looking for her. Why do I need to speak with Linnea?"

"I—I—" Incomprehension rendered her speechless. Looking at him turned her inside out. Her stomach and heart felt like they were twisted together. "I'm confused," she blurted.

He raised an eyebrow. "About what?"

"Who were you talking about then? This woman you want to propose to."

Hans smiled and reached out to touch her cheek. "Who do you think?"

Her heart pounded. "I'm learning, slowly but surely, not to make assumptions where you're concerned."

"Ah. Then let me be very clear." His eyes penetrated hers like heat. "I'm saying, Miss Barimer—Annie—I'm saying that I'm in love with you. I think I've been in love with you ever since you landed in a pile at my feet on that train." He touched her chin and chuckled softly. "Since I saw you sitting in that jail cell. Since you insisted on hauling that silly Christmas tree upstairs. And I'll probably be in love with you through a thousand more mishaps in the future. That is, if you'll allow me."

She couldn't think, couldn't formulate words to express all the thoughts that were tumbling around her head and heart. How much time had she spent thinking about him, trying to push the thoughts away, all the time not knowing he felt the same? "I had no idea."

He smiled and it took her breath away. "Now you

know. You have my heart. What are you going to do with it?''

Her heart fluttered into her throat. ''What are my choices?''

''Hmm. As I see it, you can either marry me,'' he paused dramatically while her knees turned to jelly, ''or go back to jail.''

She would have laughed if she could spare the breath. ''Please don't joke about something like this.''

''I'm not joking,'' he said, now deadly serious. ''Though I confess that jail is not really one of your options.''

''So you're saying…?''

''My third question.'' He bent down on one knee and looked up at her. ''Will you honor me by becoming my wife?''

Foolish tears filled her eyes and spilled down her cheeks. ''Are you sure?''

He clicked his tongue against his teeth but he was smiling. ''Are you going to continue to question everything I do?''

She sniffed. ''Well, you don't always use the greatest judgment.''

He laughed and stood up. ''I don't use the greatest judgment? At least I haven't gone to jail for it.''

She put her hands on her hips. ''If you did, you can be sure I wouldn't be throwing it back in your face forever.''

''Which brings me back to my question, are you going to be here forever or not?''

"It looks like I'll have to be, if only to keep you in line."

He put his hands on her shoulders. "Is that right? You need to keep me in line?"

"Yes," she said, in a rush of breath. "Even if it takes forever."

"And who's going to keep you in line?"

She raised her chin. "Fortunately, I'm quite capable of doing it myself."

"I hadn't noticed that."

She laughed. "Give me time."

He pulled her closer. "You've got all the time in the world." His face grew serious and he trailed his finger across her cheek. "Princess."

"Will they really call me that?" she asked in a voice so quiet she could barely hear it. "Is this all true?"

He nodded and pulled her close. When he lowered his mouth onto hers, she lost herself in his kiss again.

Everything about it felt right. It was like the final, most crucial piece of the puzzle of her life had finally fallen into place. She adored everything about him, she thought as she ran her hands up his back and twined her fingers into the soft hair that curled at his collar.

She was in love.

She loved the way he tasted, and the way he smelled, the way his body felt beneath her wandering fingertips. She loved the way he made her feel in his arms, like she was the most important person in the world. This was bliss and she'd waited a lifetime for it.

It was hard to believe it was finally hers.

When eventually they drew back, Hans asked, "Should we tell the girls now? I think they'll be quite pleased."

"Oh, yes. I want to tell the world," Annie said, smiling so broadly she couldn't stop.

"Not to worry, I'm sure Leo will do that."

They laughed.

"Let's go tell Besa and Marta," Annie said, eagerly anticipating the girls' reaction. They'd be thrilled, she knew. Already she could picture them in frilly little dresses for the wedding…

They walked out of the bedroom and down the beautiful marble halls that were to become Annie's home.

"Where should we go on our honeymoon?" Hans asked. "You choose. Anywhere in the world you'd like."

"Someplace the children will enjoy, too, I think," Annie said.

"The children?"

"Well, of course. We can't just leave them here alone."

"No, we'll have to get a new nanny."

"Oh, no, no, no. No daughters of mine are going to have a nanny."

"Your daughters are going to grow up 'like regular people,' right?" Hans asked with a smile.

"You betcha."

"And any more who may come along?"

A thrill ran through her. "The same."

He gave a noncommittal nod. "We'll discuss it."

"What's to discuss? As you know, I feel strongly—" She was cut off mid-sentence by a quick, silencing kiss.

In that kiss, Annie felt the lifetime of happiness that was waiting for her in Hans's arms, and her heart burst with the knowledge. After all, it wasn't every day that Prince Charming and his Cinderella bride live happily ever after.

Epilogue

From *The Washington Post,* February 14

LASSBERG, Sunday—Crown Prince Ludwig Johann Ambrose George of Kublenstein today took American Anastasia Barimer for his bride. Princess Anastasia, a former librarian at Virginia's Pendleton School for Girls, met the prince when she was hired as an English teacher for his daughters, the Princesses Marta and Besa.

"It's the most romantic story I've ever heard," said the bride's Maid of Honor, Joy Simon, interviewed on the phone from Lassberg. "I told her I had a feeling something like this was going to happen, but even I was amazed at the way things turned out." So, too, the Prince's former chief advisor, Leonard Kolbort, who has apparently resigned and taken a position with the local newspaper.

The bride wore an antique silk dress that once belonged to her grandmother. The ring was a ten-carat white diamond in a rose-gold setting, which has been worn by ten generations of royal Kublensteinian brides. She was attended by Ms. Simon, plus the royal princesses. Fifteen-hundred guests, including Princess Linnea of Borghdach, crowded into the Lorre Cathedral for the ceremony which was, apart from the bride's exclusion of the promise "to obey" her new husband, a very traditional affair.

*   *   *   *   *

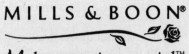

Copyright © Harlequin Enterprises Limited 1997
All rights reserved

Mills & Boon publish 29 new titles every month. Select from...

Modern Romance™   Tender Romance™

Sensual Romance™

Medical Romance™   Historical Romance™

MAT2

MILLS & BOON

Tender Romance™

HUSBANDS OF THE OUTBACK

Genni's Dilemma by Margaret Way

Genni has loved cattleman Blaine Courtland since childhood—so why is she about to marry another man...?

Charlotte's Choice by Barbara Hannay

Lady Charlotte Bellamy must accept a marriage of convenience to please her family. But her heart longs for rugged rancher Matt Lockhart...

***THE MILLIONAIRE'S DAUGHTER* by Sophie Weston**

Annis Carew knew why men pursued her – for her father's money! But gorgeous, brooding Kosta Vitale was the first man to tempt her interest. Kosta liked to be in control, but Annis unsettled him. He'd even started to think about the unthinkable—marriage!

***TO CATCH A BRIDE* by Renee Roszel**

For her grandfather's sake Kalli had agreed to marry Nikolos Varos. But when her grandfather died Kalli called off the wedding! Nikolos was furious...would he let Kalli go?

***HIS TROPHY WIFE* by Leigh Michaels**

Sloan Montgomery needed a socially acceptable wife— and revenge on the Ashworth family. So when Morganna Ashworth asked Sloan for help, he gained what he'd always wanted. But Sloan hadn't bargained on falling for his trophy wife!

On sale 6th July 2001

Available at most branches of WH Smith, Tesco, Martins, Borders, Easons, Volume One/James Thin and most good paperback bookshops

0601/02

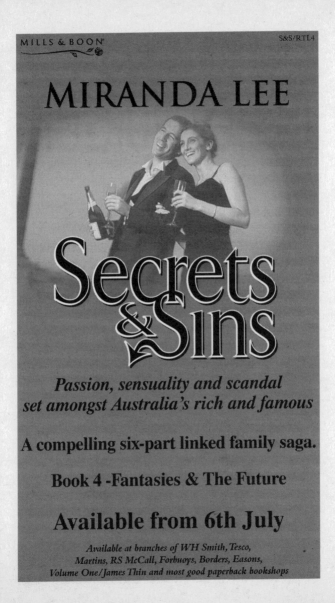

MILLS & BOON®

S&S/RTL4

MIRANDA LEE

Secrets & Sins

*Passion, sensuality and scandal
set amongst Australia's rich and famous*

A compelling six-part linked family saga.

Book 4 -Fantasies & The Future

Available from 6th July

*Available at branches of WH Smith, Tesco,
Martins, RS McCall, Forbuoys, Borders, Easons,
Volume One/James Thin and most good paperback bookshops*

MILLS & BOON®

0501/114/MB13

IN HOT PURSUIT

Nat, Mark and Michael are three sexy men, each in pursuit of the woman they intend to have...at all costs!

Three brand-new stories for a red-hot summer read!

**Vicki Lewis Thompson
Sherry Lewis
Roz Denny Fox**

Published 18th May

*Available at branches of WH Smith, Tesco,
Martins, RS McCall, Forbuoys, Borders, Easons,
Sainsbury, Woolworth and most good paperback bookshops*

MILLS & BOON®

STEEP/RTL/3

The STEEPWOOD
Scandal

*REGENCY DRAMA, INTRIGUE,
MISCHIEF ... AND MARRIAGE*

A new collection of 16 linked
Regency Romances, set in the villages
surrounding Steepwood Abbey.

Book 3
The Reluctant Bride
by Meg Alexander

Available 6th July

*Available at branches of WH Smith, Tesco,
Martins, RS McCall, Forbuoys, Borders, Easons,
Sainsbury, Woolworth and most good paperback bookshops*

Modern Romance™

Eight brand new titles each month

...seduction and
passion guaranteed

Available at most branches of WH Smith, Tesco,
Martins, Borders, Easons, Volume One/James Thin
and most good paperback bookshops

GEN/01/RTL2

Medical Romance™

Six brand new titles each month

...*medical drama on the pulse.*

Available at most branches of WH Smith, Tesco, Martins, Borders, Easons, Volume One/James Thin and most good paperback bookshops

GEN/03/RTL2

FREE
2 BOOKS
AND A SURPRISE GIFT!

We would like to take this opportunity to thank you for reading this Mills & Boon® book by offering you the chance to take TWO more specially selected titles from the Tender Romance™ series absolutely FREE! We're also making this offer to introduce you to the benefits of the Reader Service™—

★ FREE home delivery   ★ FREE gifts and competitions
★ FREE monthly Newsletter   ★ Exclusive Reader Service discounts
★ Books available before they're in the shops

Accepting these FREE books and gift places you under no obligation to buy; you may cancel at any time, even after receiving your free shipment. Simply complete your details below and return the entire page to the address below. *You don't even need a stamp!*

YES! Please send me 2 free Tender Romance books and a surprise gift. I understand that unless you hear from me, I will receive 4 superb new titles every month for just £2.49 each, postage and packing free. I am under no obligation to purchase any books and may cancel my subscription at any time. The free books and gift will be mine to keep in any case.

N1ZEC

Ms/Mrs/Miss/Mr ....Initials ....
BLOCK CAPITALS PLEASE
Surname ....
Address ....
....
....Postcode ....

Send this whole page to:
UK: FREEPOST CN81, Croydon, CR9 3WZ
EIRE: PO Box 4546, Kilcock, County Kildare (stamp required)

Offer valid in UK and Eire only and not available to current Reader Service subscribers to this series. We reserve the right to refuse an application and applicants must be aged 18 years or over. Only one application per household. Terms and prices subject to change without notice. Offer expires 31st December 2001. As a result of this application, you may receive further offers from Harlequin Mills & Boon Limited and other carefully selected companies. If you would prefer not to share in this opportunity please write to The Data Manager at the address above.

Mills & Boon® is a registered trademark owned by Harlequin Mills & Boon Limited.
Tender Romance™ is being used as a trademark.